HEART OF DORKNESS

And Other Stories

HENRY VOGEL

Published in the United States of America by Rampant Loon Press, an imprint of Rampant Loon Media LLC, P.O. Box 111, Lake Elmo, Minnesota 55042. "Rampant Loon Press" and the Rampant Loon colophon are trademarks of Rampant Loon Media LLC.

www.rampantloonmedia.com

Cover by Miblart.com

ISBN: 978-1-958333-07-5 (ebook)

ISBN: 978-1-958333-06-8 (paperback)

First publication: February, 2025

For my sister-in-law Anne, who has been a haven of support and sanity for me since Audrey, her sister and my wife, died.

HEART OF DORKNESS

The con had wound down. The fans had all gone back to their mundane lives, leaving the five of us in the con suite. Our host, the Gaming Director, passed around what was left of the free sodas. We drank and stared out the window as darkness gathered in the skies above the hotel. The Power Gamer spoke of adventures long past, with the Rules Lawyer interrupting whenever the Power Gamer incorrectly stated a rule. The rest of us listened, extending the camaraderie of the con just a bit longer.

As the Power Gamer wound down, Marlow took over the narrative. "Ah, friend, you have put me in mind of ancient games and old times. Of when Third Edition conquered the gaming realms, banishing our cherished characters as mere second edition cardboard characters. The end of the era when all it took was a handful of dice and a few spare minutes to bring your character to life."

We all lifted our soda cans in salute to the bygone age as Marlow continued. "To learn this new approach to gaming, many of us of ventured forth to small cons, far from the great cities and grand hotels of the major cons. I was among those who ventured far from game shops, far from comic book stores, far from civilization itself. I remember not the name of the con, just that my dear aunt was on the con committee and could get me in for free. Friends, a free con does not mean a good con. Let this serve as a warning to you.

"The con was held in a small motel with only three floors. As I waited in line to register, I wondered how anyone could gain the true con experience without the long wait for an elevator or the frustration of missing a cherished event because it was too far from the gaming tables to visit between rounds. They got one part of the experience right. The registration line was painfully slow! Yet after that promising start, events spiraled ever downward.

"Emerging at last from the registration line, I was prepared to rush to the game room to register for all the good adventures. But my dear aunt grabbed me at the last second. Members of the 501st Legion of Stormtroopers had to be guided to the Star Wars room. From there, I was pressed into service, dropping a band of elven warriors off at the Lord of the Rings room. From there, I took Spider-Man to the superhero room, then guided goths to the Vampire LARP. By the time I escaped from con committee supervision and reached the gaming room, all the first round games but one were filled. I read the adventure description. 'A band of adventurers travel down a river into the heart of the Orc lands to rescue a great warrior and bring him to the safety of the lawful lands.' It sounded like an exciting adventure. I quickly signed up for it and, as the first round of games was about to begin, went in search of the table.

"I should have known there was a problem when I saw the way the gamemaster was dressed. He wore khaki pants, an Oxford shirt, and loafers. At a *con*, no less. But I foolishly assumed he hadn't done his laundry recently, and that's why he was stuck with inappropriate con attire. As I was the last player to arrive, the gamemaster passed out character sheets as soon as I sat down. Before looking at the character sheet, I started setting up for serious gaming; getting out my first round dice, arranging paper and my pen, the typical approach for any gamer. This met with the disapproval of the gamemaster. 'You should read your character sheet immediately. You have much to learn before we begin.'

"I looked at the character sheet, and revised that to character sheets. The guy had written six pages of information about the character! All the important stuff was at the beginning, or so I thought. I was a good fighter but could sail a boat due to blah blah blah blah. The gamemaster used two pages just explaining how my character learned seamanship. Those two pages even included why my character disliked tuna! By now, the other players and I were casting glances back and forth, wondering what we had gotten ourselves into. We soon learned.

"The six characters had been hired to take a boat up river into Orc lands to rescue the mighty warrior, just as the adventure description said. As boat's captain, I ordered everyone to the boat so we could cast off. 'No, you can't,' the gamemaster told me. 'The boat is badly in need of repairs.' I just stared at the gamemaster, then said, 'Fine. We repair the boat, then cast off.' The gamemaster frowned and shook his head, 'You don't have enough nails to do the job.'

"And so we spent the first 30 minutes of the game trying to buy enough nails to repair the ship. We had a dwarf in the group and tried to have him strike a deal with local dwarven smiths. But, no, that we could not do. In this land, dwarves were farmers, not smiths. I could not believe what I was hearing! Dwarven farmers? By the gods! But the nails were not the end of the foolishness. Upon completing our repairs, we found a large band of Orcs had slipped onto the boat. This, I thought, was more like it! 'I draw my sword and attack the Orcs,' I said. The gamemaster did it to me again. 'No, you don't,' he said. 'This is the crew you hired to help sail the boat upriver.'

"We all stared at the gamemaster in disbelief. 'I hired a crew?' I asked. 'Yes,' he replied. 'Of Orcs,' I asked. 'Yes,' he replied. 'I did this knowing a dwarf was a member of the crew? A dwarf whose racial enemy is Orcs?' I asked again. 'Oh, that!' the gamemaster replied. 'The dwarf was raised by kindly Orc farmers after his parents died in the plague. The dwarf has quite a friendly disposition towards Orcs.' This was too much for the player with the dwarf. 'I have a friendly disposition towards Orcs?' he cried. 'I did not see that on my character sheet.' The gamemaster merely smiled. 'Yet it is there. Look at appendix B, footnote four.' The dwarven player rifled through his character sheet. When his head fell into his hands, we knew the gamemaster had won the point.

"Our band set forth to sail the river. And we discovered our little boat was a steamboat rather than a sailing boat. The gamemaster prepared himself for an argument, but we accepted the steam engine. Fantasy sometimes features steam power along with magical power. Besides, we thought the steam engine would let us reach the real adventure area quickly. After an hour of finding nails, fixing the boat, and arguing over Orc crewmen, I assure you were all prepared to do battle against hordes of Orcs. It didn't work that way.

"The gamemaster spent the next hour and a half narrating our journey upstream in excruciating detail. He described the plants on the river banks. He described the rancid meat the Orcs ate in such detail I lost my appetite for lunch! He described the villages we passed. He even described the number of mosquito bites our characters received and how badly the bites itched. Then, finally, after what felt like forever, our boat was attacked by savage Orcs! At last, we players thought, a call to action!

"I told the gamemaster, 'I draw my sword and leap to attack the closest Orc!' The gamemaster frowned in disapproval telling me, 'There is another way to deal with this!' Through clenched teeth, I repeated, 'I draw my sword and leap to attack the closest Orc!' The gamemaster gave me a piercing stare, as if willing me to find this other way of which he spoke. I stared right back as I rolled for initiative. 'I got a 13 for initiative,' I announced.

Throwing his hands up, the gamemaster said, 'Fine. Ruin the adventure. It's your loss!'

"For the next thirty minutes, we players actually had fun. Not as much fun as we could have had, as the gamemaster gave only the barest of descriptions of the combat. There was no spurting blood or hacked off limbs, just 'You hit, roll damage' repeated in a monotone. All too soon, the battle was over and our cleric set about healing us. My character spoke to the Orc crew, 'Gather up the bodies, boys! Fresh meat is back on your menu!' The gamemaster snarled, 'Your character wouldn't say that!' I snarled back, 'He just did!' The gamemaster made a note, 'That's going to cost you experience points for playing out of character. And why did you fight the Orcs? You could have scared them away by simply sounding the steam whistle!' After the six of us had scraped our jaws off the table, I replied, 'Because it is more fun to fight!' The gamemaster actually tilted his head back to make sure his nose was in position to look down and said, 'Oh, I see. You are a group of roll players rather than role players.' You could just hear the double L in roll, too.

"It was at that time our gamemaster gave us the first good news of our adventure. 'So much time was lost in the fruitless battle with the Orcs,' he told us, 'I am forced to rush your journey upriver. Much flavor will be lost.' Smiles broke out all around. Our fight had earned us a fast trip to the rescue of the mighty warrior! The gamemaster brushed over the next ten days of travel, ten days I believe would have taken an hour and a half for him to complete!

"Soon we were bringing the boat to the riverside, ready for an exciting rescue. Before we left the boat, we tied up the Orc crew so they wouldn't simply steal the boat. This course of action did not sit well with the gamemaster. 'No, no, no!' he protested, looking at our dwarven player. 'Your character would not allow these Orcs to be so mistreated!' The dwarven player, his jaw firmly set, replied, 'My dwarf is on the deck, whistling loudly. He hears nothing, suspects nothing, does nothing.' Oh, did the gamemaster rant and rail about that, though he knew there was little he could do to force the issue.

"Moments later, we slipped into the jungle beside the river, moving toward a hilltop fire. We heard chanting coming from the hilltop. Perhaps the mighty warrior was about to be sacrificed to an evil Orc god! Anticipating a good fight, we hurried ahead. And literally tripped over a human man as he lay watching the Orc ceremony. 'Kurtz the warrior, I presume,' I said. All hopes of a daring rescue collapsed when the man answered, 'Aye, Kurtz, I am. You are the men sent to rescue me?' At our nods, the man looked toward the fire, 'longly' the gamemaster told us, then said, 'I do not wish to leave this... this... ceremony, gentlemen. It beckons, drawing me toward it.'

"I cast a glance at the other players, 'I suspect Kurtz is bespelled. We shall not draw him from this evil place while the spell still stands.' Looking at the gamemaster, who was about to say something, I loudly proclaimed, 'Drawing my sword, I charge into the clearing and attack the nearest Orc!' I knew I had done the right thing as the gamemaster had despair written all over his face. 'No!' he said. 'He's not bespelled! Kurtz simply longs to join the uncivilized simplicity of the native culture!' I cut him off. 'The Orcs are obviously caught flatfooted. We all get a free attack before they can react!' Ah, the protests and wails of the gamemaster ring in my ears still. It wasn't much of a fight, but it was worth it simply to hear him wail and complain.

"Two combat rounds later, the Orc bodies littered the ground. As we searched the bodies, Kurtz charged into the clearing, screaming at us. We all knew the gamemaster was just using Kurtz as a way of yelling at us. We also noted the gamemaster had not had Kurtz draw his sword. We waited until he reached us, then all attacked at once. Oh, the look on the gamemaster's face! It was worth the entire excuse for an adventure! Kurtz did not live to draw his blade again. We looted his body as well, then returned to the boat. Once there, we slaughtered the Orc crew, looted their bodies and set sail back down the river.

"We got no farther, as the gamemaster completely lost his composure. 'You cretins! You morons! I spent over a year designing this adventure, drawing from one of the great works of English literature!' he ranted. 'I thought I could bring culture to the likes of you! I should have known better!' By this time, the entire gaming room had gone quiet as everyone turned to watch our table.

"Perhaps I should have let the gamemaster stalk out with the last word, yet I did not. 'What great work of literature was the adventure based upon?' I asked. All energy seemed to have flowed out of the gamemaster. He answered quietly, 'It was Heart of Darkness.' The other players all looked confused. Obviously, they did not recognize the story. I took pity on them and said, 'Heart of Darkness is part of the second dark elf trilogy that TSR published back before Wizards of the Coast bought them.' For some reason, the gamemaster cried, 'The horror! The horror!' and ran from the gaming room. I looked at my fellow players, 'The gamemaster is right. The dark elf trilogy is one of the great works of English literature.'"

The Gaming Director looked out the window again. Darkness completely covered the hotel. It was time to leave. Time to return to the mundane world, just as all the others had done. Standing, he said, "Wow, it's a pity the guy did such a terrible job of converting the dark elf stuff. That could have been an adventure for the ages."

We all nodded sagely, filing from the con suite. The Gaming Director hit the light switch and closed the door. Behind us, darkness claimed the heart of the con.

WATCH THIS!

"Hey, Cletus, hold my beer and watch this!"

That was the last thing Ronnie remembered saying before he ended up... wherever it was he'd ended up. He was standing in a line of some kind. A long line. And a real quiet one, too. Briefly, he wondered what the line was for, got bored with that, and started looking around.

All he saw to his right was bright and white that seemed to go on forever. Bo-o-o-o-oring! On his left, he spied some kind of high fence. It looked like wrought iron or something else expensive. On the other side of the fence was a high shrub wall, so he couldn't see what was inside the fence. Behind him was Cletus. And the rest of the line.

"Damn, now that's one long line!" Ronnie said.

"You want your beer back, Ronnie?" Cletus asked, holding out the open can of PBR.

Ronnie took the beer, glad to see Cletus had held onto the twelve pack after whatever had happened. That was one thing you could count on from Cletus. He *always* held onto the beer. That's why he was Ronnie's best friend in the entire world.

Ronnie had no idea what was going on, but he was sure it was going to be easier to face after a few beers. Draining the warm

PBR in one long pull, Ronnie belched loudly, crushed the can on his forehead, and tossed the empty over his shoulder. Faces turned toward them, frowning at Ronnie and Cletus. Taking another beer from Cletus, Ronnie tried frowning back. Everyone else just turned away. Not one of them asked for a beer.

"Cletus, we ain't in Kansas no more!"

"Ronnie, I ain't never been to Kansas afore, so there ain't no way we ain't in Kansas no more. You gots to be in a place 'fore you can't be in it no more!"

That was another thing Ronnie liked about Cletus. Cletus made Ronnie feel smart, and there weren't many people he could say that about.

"You got any idea what this line is for?" Ronnie asked Cletus.

"Can't be for beer or someone woulda asked us for one," Cletus replied, "unless they don't like PBR."

Ronnie tapped the person in front of him on the shoulder.

"Hey, you know what this here line is for?"

The person brushed his shoulder off, frowned even more deeply than when Ronnie had belched and turned away.

"Only one thing could get this many people out to stand in line on the 4th of July, Cletus. Got to be a concert!"

"Could be a white sale, Ronnie," Cletus said. "My momma told some real horror stories 'bout lines at white sales."

Ronnie rolled his eyes and said, "You got any money on you?"

Turning out his pockets, Cletus replied, "Nope."

"Me neither," said Ronnie. "Dang, how we gonna get into this here concert without any money?"

"Do what we always do, Ronnie," Cletus said. "Pull the truck up to the fence and we can hop over."

"Good thinking, Cletus!" Ronnie said. "You remember where we parked the truck?"

"Heck, Ronnie, I don't even remember driving here!" Cletus replied.

"Aw, Hell."

Again, faces turned toward Ronnie, frowning the deepest

frown yet. Ronnie flipped them off and pulled Cletus from the line.

"Gimme a boost up to the top of the fence. Then I'll pull you up," he told Cletus.

"What about the beer, Ronnie?"

"Well, of course you're gonna hand the beer up to me first! You think I'm gonna leave perfectly good beer for these people?" Ronnie waved his hand toward the line.

The people in the line watched as Cletus boosted Ronnie to the top of the fence. As Cletus handed the beer to Ronnie, one man in the line turned to another.

"Shouldn't we stop them?" he asked.

"Not my problem," replied the other man. "Besides, the guy behind me probably wouldn't let us back in line."

"I beg your pardon?" said the man behind him. "Unlike those morons, you surely know why we're in this line! I am honest and trustworthy or I wouldn't be here."

"Yeah, yeah. After you get through the gates, I'll believe you. Right now, you're just another guy who's nervous about the big interview coming up. Besides, the morons are already over the fence."

Dropping to the ground inside the fence, Ronnie and Cletus looked around. Expecting an amphitheater, they found themselves looking at a city with streets of gold and buildings of gold, silver and marble. It was the most amazing sight either of had ever seen. It kept their attention for almost fifteen seconds.

"Don't see no concert, Ronnie," Cletus said, opening another PBR.

"Good thing you told me, Cletus, 'cause I'd never have figgered it out," Ronnie replied, his words thick with sarcasm.

"That's what friends are for, Ronnie," Cletus said, completely missing the sarcasm.

"All right, now be quiet. Maybe we can hear the crowd or something if we listen hard," said Ronnie.

Both men listened hard, interrupted only be the occasional swig of beer. After a minute, Cletus spoke.

"Hey, I hear something, Ronnie! Over that a way!"

And now Ronnie could hear it, too. It didn't sound like rock or country or even bluegrass, but it was music. After making sure Cletus still had the beer, Ronnie led off toward the music. After a bit of walking, they found the amphitheater.

"Told you it was a concert," Ronnie said. "People don't line up like that for anything else!"

"Where we gonna sit, Ronnie?"

"Down front, of course! Just follow me and act natural like," Ronnie told him.

"Okay," Cletus replies, following his friend.

"Ronnie?" Cletus asked after a few seconds.

"Yeah, Cletus?" Ronnie replied.

"How would I act if I didn't act natural like?"

"You know, unnatural like," Ronnie said.

"Well, what's unnatural like? So's I don't act that way," Cletus asked.

Ronnie sighed. "Trying to kiss me would be unnatural, Cletus."

"Oh," Cletus said, nodding. "I won't try to kiss you, Ronnie."

"Shut up, Cletus. I think they're about to start something new."

Ronnie was right. Music swelled around them, unlike anything Ronnie and Cletus had ever heard before. The music was cosmic. It was primal. It was triumphant. It was soothing. It was soul-stirring and spirit uplifting.

It was not *Free Bird*.

Polishing off another beer, Ronnie yelled, "Free Bird!"

Cletus joined in, "Free Bird!"

The music ground to a halt. All around them, faces turned toward them, expressions of indescribable joy vanishing behind deep frowns. Ronnie and Cletus remained oblivious.

"Free Bird!" they yelled together. "Free Bird!"

Then, with a flash of light, the amphitheater vanished from around Ronnie and Cletus. They found themselves facing a crowd of angry people, all talking at once to... Ronnie gaped. The angry people were all talking to God. And they were all pointing at him. And at Cletus, but not as much.

God lifted one hand, and silence fell. His great eyes turned toward Ronnie and Ronnie wanted to hide behind Cletus.

"It appears," God's voice rang out, "that discord has entered the realm of Heaven. Entered on sneaker-clad feet."

"Uh, what's He mean, Ronnie?" Cletus whispered.

"He means we pissed off a lot of people, Cletus," Ronnie whispered back.

"There is no need to whisper, Cletus," God said. "I hear all, regardless of volume."

"Ronnie," Cletus sounded nervous, "He knows my name!"

"Course He knows your name, dumbass. God knows everything!" Ronnie told him.

"I know He knows everything. I just figgered it was important stuff. My name ain't important."

"It is to me, Cletus, just as you are important to me," God said. "Another important question is how the two of you came to be here."

"Ronnie," Cletus whispered again, "I thought you said God knows everything?"

"I do, Cletus," God said, "but confession is good for the soul. Trust me on this."

"We, uh," Ronnie began, "we climbed over your fence, sir. I mean, your Godliness. And we went to a concert."

"Which you interrupted with repeated calls for *Free Bird*," God added. "While Ronnie Van Zant will be pleased to know his work is still appreciated on earth, I would like for you to start a bit earlier. Let Us say, shortly before you asked Cletus to hold your beer."

"Oh, yeah, Ronnie! You got to tell Him about that!" Cletus said.

Ronnie squirmed as all eyes turned, again, toward him.

"Well," Ronnie began, "my cousin Billy got his hands on some real good stuff for lighting grills. And, you know, it being the 4th of July, I figgered I'd use it to start the fire for my cook out. I poured a whole bunch of the stuff over my charcoal and-"

"What kind of 'stuff' was it, Ronnie?" God asked.

"Well, You know, sir. God."

"Yes, I do. As does Peter, as the act is now recorded in the Book of Life. But none of these others know."

"It, uh, was, uh, some jet fuel and, uh, something cousin Billy said was liquid oxygen. He said it would burn something fierce," Ronnie continued.

"So, I, uh, poured a bunch of both on my charcoal. Then I asked Cletus to hold my beer. I lit a match. And then we were outside your fence."

Comprehension suddenly pushed its way through the fog of beer in Ronnie's mind.

"Ah, man, I'm real sorry, Cletus! I killed you with my grill!" Ronnie said, distraught.

"That's okay, Ronnie," Cletus said. "I ain't mad or nothing. And it that grill lighting was something to see!"

"Peter?" God asked.

"Yes, my Lord?" replied an old man with a long beard.

"Take Ronnie and Cletus and bring them into My realm properly, please."

"You mean I ain't going to Hell?" Ronnie asked. "I mean, I killed my best friend!"

"I done told you I ain't upset about that, Ronnie," Cletus said.

A book suddenly appeared in Peter's hands. "Ronald Roosevelt Jenkins, you have led an aimless life, but one filled with kindness toward others. Accidentally killing your best friend was not a good way to end your life, but your friend's forgiveness counts in your favor."

Peter looked up, and the book vanished. "You are to be welcomed into the Kingdom of Heaven, Ronald."

"Ronnie," God said, just before Peter led the two men away, "you are not the first to say 'Hold my beer and watch this!' Nor will you be the last. In a way, you are hard-wired to say such things."

"I don't understand, sir. Um, my Lord," Ronnie said.

God smiled at him. "Do you know your Bible well, Ronnie?"

"Pretty well. I think," Ronnie replied.

"In Genesis, do you recall the words I spoke when creating the heavens and the earth?"

"Oh, I know!" Cletus exclaimed. "You said 'Let there be light' and there was light!"

"Very good, Cletus," God said. "But I edited that a bit before sending My divine inspiration. My first words were..."

Even Peter's eyes widened in surprise and anticipation.

"...Hey, Lucifer! Hold my nectar and watch this!"

JOHN CARTER AND THE BRONZE MEN IN MARS

W ere it not for the potency of Barsoomian wine, none of what I tell you now would have happened. Yet even then, Tars Tarkas and I almost foiled the kidnapping. Though it seems as if it were just yesterday, these events began nearly one Barsoomian year ago. Tar Tarkas took advantage of my standing invitation to visit Dejah Thoris and me, bringing barrels of wine he purchased along the way. Great was the feasting, and many were the tales of brave deeds. As the evening wore on, those of lesser constitution succumbed to the wine and left for their sleeping furs. Last to depart was my incomparable Dejah Thoris.

"Hail, Tars Tarkas, and good night," she spoke formally, as befitted our guest's noble rank. Turning to me, she smiled, "I shall leave you two old warriors to your wine and your stories. Join me in our sleeping furs when you grow tired, my chieftain."

Left to ourselves, the six-limbed Jeddak of Thark and the Warlord of Barsoom returned to our reminiscing. Greatest among our regrets was that there was nothing new to discover on Barsoom; no forgotten civilizations, no ancient enmities. There is still a great need for men of action such as ourselves, for war is like a religion to all races of Barsoom. Yet the sense of discovery, that fine spice that adds so much to the flavor of adventure, was gone. Little did we know how quickly life would prove us wrong!

As Tars Tarkas and I spent a final few minutes silently enjoying the wine and the pleasure of the other's company, an unusual sound intruded upon the silence. It was not loud and lesser men might have put it to wind or some other natural source. Yet the giant green warrior and I recognized the sound for what it was; the gentle rasp of a sword sliding from its scabbard!

In a bound I was across the room and through the door, where I beheld the only sight which can instill fear within my breast. On the far side of the hall, a bronze-colored man wearing harnesses I did not recognize carried the limp form of my love, Dejah Thoris, heading into an unused section of our house. Before me, blocking my path, stood three unkempt men, also colored of bronze. They wore no harnesses, but each one wielded a long sword. By their stances, it was obvious they knew how to use the weapons. Only the height of the ceiling kept me from using my earthly muscles to leap over the three men and pursue the abductor.

I observed all of this in the blink of an eye. Then, never one to shy from action, attacked the three swordsmen before me. You may think me rash to take on three armed men and, in truth, they sorely pressed me. Yet such is my love for the incomparable Dejah Thoris that I will face such odds and worse to return her to my side!

As I wove a web of steel between myself and my unknown opponents, I studied them. I had never seen such bronze coloring on any man of Barsoom. Despite their unkempt appearance, the men were all well formed, lean and strong. Within their eyes burned such haughty pride that I knew they felt themselves superior to me in every way. As the seconds passed and the three of them failed to land a blow upon me, that pride faded, replaced by growing respect for my fighting prowess.

"Stand aside," I told them. "There is no shame in recognizing and giving way to the better man. Allow me to pass and you have my word you will suffer no harm!"

In answer, the three men redoubled their efforts. They forced me back one step, two steps. Then I drew upon the indomitable will that sustains me and stood fast, refusing to retreat further. Though I longed to be off in pursuit of Dejah Thoris, I gloried in the thrill I always get from fighting and felt my old, familiar smile play across my lips.

Suddenly, Tars Tarkas joined in the fray. Unable to cross a room in a single bound, he had spent precious seconds running across the banquet hall to join me. With my friend battling at my side, we pressed the attack. The three bronze men gave way by a step, then two, then they were moving steadily backward under our relentless attack. A faltered step left a small opening in their combined defense. My blade flashed and one bronze man dropped lifelessly to the floor. Fighting one on one against two of Barsoom's mightiest warriors, the remaining two bronze men soon joined their companion.

As the last man had dropped to the floor, I race across the hall after the abductor and my beloved Dejah Thoris. I dashed through one unused room, then another. In the third room, I found a something unexpected; a hole in the floor! As I have always preferred action to deliberation, I immediately leaped into the hole. Within, I discovered a tunnel sloping down into darkness. Somehow, there was light coming from the other end of the tunnel, far away though it was. I saw small shapes moving against the light. Knowing this to be the abductor, I set off in pursuit.

As I ran, I called over my shoulder, "Tars Tarkas! The hole is but one end of a tunnel. I fear the tunnel is too low for you, my friend!"

"Where goes John Carter," came the mighty Thark's reply, "so also goes Tars Tarkas!"

Casting a quick glance over my shoulder, I saw my friend

enter the tunnel using his mid-limbs as legs. He ran forward as quickly as I, easily fitting into the tunnel. It gladdened my heart to know my fierce friend would be at my side as I faced what lay before me.

Our pursuit wore on and on, and the tunnel turned out to be far longer than I had imagined. Minute piled on passing minute, and still the tunnel stretched out before us. Despite the distance run, my pace did not slacken, for she who was more important than life itself was counting on me. Nor did Tars Tarkas flag in his pursuit. Slowly, we gained on those ahead of us. Too slowly, for I saw they would escape the tunnel before we would catch them. Mere minutes later, they did just that.

Two minutes that seemed more like two years passed before Tars Tarkas and I emerged from the mouth of the tunnel. Half blinded by sunlight brighter than any I had ever seen on Barsoom, I could barely see the abductor carry my beloved Dejah Thoris into a waiting flyer. As the flyer rose into the air, I gathered all of my strength for a mighty leap; a leap which would have carried me onto the rising flyer!

Just as I was about to spring, a weighted net came down on top of Tars Tarkas and me. Men piled on top of us from all sides, pummeling us with the flats of their blades. I had just time to watch the flyer sail off into the distance before all went black.

I came to with the suddenness known to all men of action. Straining my senses, I attempted to learn all I could of my surroundings without opening my eyes. The sounds of harsh laughter and vulgar conversation came to my ears. The smell of unwashed bodies invaded my nose. I felt an oppressive heat upon my skin and coarse rope around my wrists and ankles.

"Keep your eyes closed for now," a voice murmured from nearby. "Kroulk does not yet know you are awake. When you speak, try to keep your lips still."

"Who are you?" I asked quietly and carefully.

"The closest thing you have to a friend in this camp," came the reply.

"What of my friend, Tars Tarkas?"

"If you speak of the giant green man, he lies not three feet from you, trussed more thoroughly than you," said the unknown man. "It took many men to subdue him. Kroulk is taking no chances that the green warrior will get free."

"Where on Barsoom are we?"

A soft laugh, then, "You are not *on* Barsoom, you are *in* it!"

There are some things no man can hear without a reaction. Such was the stranger's response. With a start, I opened my eyes. Despite what I had just heard, my mind almost refused to accept what I saw. I looked toward the horizon only to discover there was no horizon! Instead, the world before me curved *up* toward the distant sky.

I put aside contemplation of this strange world for now. It has always been thus for me. The call for decisive action overrides all else, even the wonder of a world within a world! My gaze swept the crude camp and its brutish men, coming to rest on a man sitting near to me. He was unlike the other men I had seen. An old campaigner such as myself could easily recognize a man who strove to present as neat an appearance as possible under hard conditions. Where the harnesses of the other men were grimy, his gleamed. Where their hair fell in greasy tangles, his was clean and combed. Where dirt covered their bodies, he was well scrubbed. The strangely bronze colored skin was the only similarity between my friend and the other men in the camp.

My open eyes had attracted attention. A large, hulking man whose eyes shone with cruelty and contempt was swaggering toward us. The contrast in appearance between this brute and my new friend could not have been greater. A single glance told me this man took pride in his disgusting appearance and felt only contempt for one who did not follow his example.

"So, Shom Kerr," the brute growled, "the prisoner is awake. Did I not give orders to be told as soon as he awoke?"

"He has only just done so, Kroulk," Shom Kerr told him.

Kroulk's foot lashed out, catching Shom Kerr on the side of the head.

"*Jeddak* Kroulk!" he bellowed.

The claim was so ridiculous, I could not help but to laugh, "Jeddak? Of what? This excuse for a camp?"

Kroulk's face screwed up in rage and his foot lashed out at my head. Tied though I was, I rolled just out of range of the blow. As his foot sailed past me, I spun just enough so I could kick Kroulk's foot from beneath. With a satisfying thump, Kroulk landed on his back. Laughter, harsh and unsympathetic, rose from the men behind Kroulk. Jumping quickly to his feet, Kroulk eyed me with open hatred.

"For that, surface scum, you die!" Kroulk proclaimed to the cheers of the men behind him.

I returned Kroulk's gaze levelly, "Give me a sword, Kroulk, and we will see which of us dies this day!"

As I was looking him straight in the eye, only I saw the fear that flashed in Kroulk's eyes. I knew then that he would take the coward's way.

"A warrior's death?" Kroulk sneered. "The likes of you do not deserve such an honor!"

Murmuring arose from the men behind Kroulk and he knew his position, probably his very life, hung on his next action. Kroulk did as all tyrants do when their bullying ways fail them; he offered his followers blood as entertainment.

"Shom Kerr," Kroulk said loudly, "take your knife and slit this man's throat. Then slit the throat of his green friend!"

The men met this declaration with raucous cheers from the rest of the camp. Eyes downcast, Shom Kerr moved in front of me, drawing his dagger.

"I fear I have but one choice of action, my friend," Shom Kerr said, his eyes rising to meet mine. A smile played across his lips—the smile of a warrior born, ready for battle to begin. With a quick slash, Shom Kerr's dagger parted the rope binding my wrists.

Placing the dagger in my hand, Shom Kerr said, "Free yourself and your friend. I will hold these brutes off while you escape!"

Drawing his sword, Shom Kerr rose to face a stunned Kroulk. I wasted no time cutting through the rope around my ankles, then turned to help Tars Tarkas. I found his eyes open and the same warrior's smile played out across his lipless mouth. It was the work of but a second to part the cords binding the great Thark's upper hands. As Shom Kerr had done, I placed the dagger in Tars Tarkas's hand. Rising, I looked for our weapons. I spied them leaning against a rock on the far side of the camp. Too far away for a Barsoomian to reach, the weapons were but a single bound away for a man born in earth's greater gravity!

My leap stunned all in the camp, save Tars Tarkas. No one moved as I grabbed our weapons and bounded back to my now-freed companion. Swords drawn, we took our place on either side of Shom Kerr, who pressed Kroulk sorely.

"To me!" Kroulk called to his men, fear evident in his voice. "Your Jeddak commands you! To me!"

A handful of the coarser men rushed to join Kroulk. Tars Tarkas and I laid into them and soon their bodies littered the ground. At the sight of this, the other men backed away fearfully, none reaching for a sword.

"Come, you cowards!" Kroulk tried again, the fear now evident on his face. "They are but three! If you all attack, we can overwhelm them!"

"Enough of this," Shom Kerr declared. "You do not deserve a warrior's death, but I tire of your cowardly, bullying ways!"

At that, Shom Kerr's blade flashed with such speed and skill as I have seen but a few times in my long life. In seconds, Kroulk lay on the ground, Shom Kerr's sword impaled in his heart.

Turning his back on the rest of the men, Shom Kerr said to

me, "You have reminded me of a warrior's honor, my friend. To whom do I owe thanks?"

Tars Tarkas spoke then, "Know you not the greatest warrior ever to stride the sands of Barsoom? Know you not he whom all have proclaimed the Warlord of Barsoom? Know you not John Carter, Prince of Helium?"

"Even here, within Barsoom, we have heard tales of John Carter," Shom Kerr said. "Given the deeds ascribed to you, I expected you to be much taller!"

I laughed, "I am sure the tales are greatly exaggerated, Shom Kerr."

Shom Kerr's eye measured the distance I had leaped to retrieve the weapons and said, "I am not so sure of that, John Carter."

With the dry laugh of his people, Tars Tarkas said, "If anything, the tales cannot do justice to John Carter's exploits!"

Putting aside this talk of my great deeds, which no true warrior dwells upon, I gestured toward the rest of men, "What of these men, Shom Kerr? This is your land. We will defer to your ways."

Shom Kerr's eyes swept across the men. "They are not bad men, John Carter, only badly led. Allow me to speak with them."

Shom Kerr walked over to the men and began speaking in low, reasonable tones. While he did so, Tars Tarkas and I cleaned our weapons. Moments later, Shom Kerr returned. Behind him, the men slowly drifted into the forest around the clearing.

"Where are they going?" I asked.

"To bathe, to clean their harnesses, to make themselves presentable as men of Mordon, our country, should be," Shom Kerr told me. "But what of you, John Carter? I assume you were chasing those who took the woman from the surface world?"

"You are correct, Shom Kerr," I told him. "The woman is my wife, Dejah Thoris, and I shall not rest until she is returned to my side! Perhaps one of your men can take a message from me through the tunnel to Tardos Mors, Jeddak of Helium and grandfather of Dejah Thoris. He can have an army of Heliumites here within a day!"

"That is not possible, John Carter," Shom Kerr told me, "for the tunnel is no longer there."

"How can the tunnel be gone?" I asked, astounded. "Surely, Tars Tarkas and I were not unconscious long enough for you to fill in the entire tunnel!"

"No tunnel was dug," Shom Kerr told me. "A device controlled by Jorn Sook, tyrant Jeddak of Mordon, created it. The device isolates the second ray from the core of Barsoom, creating a tunnel where none existed before and where none exists after the device is switched off. It is that device that has allowed rulers of Mordon to take slaves from the surface world without giving away our presence. It is that device which has trapped you here for all time!"

"If you think that," Tars Tarkas said, "you do not know John Carter!"

"While I yet live, there is hope!" I said.

A sad smiled crossed Shom Kerr's lips, and he whispered, "Oh, Bel Ahn, you would like this John Carter. Indeed, you would."

"Who is Bel Ahn?" I asked.

"My love, and the reason I am here," Shom Kerr told me. "Jorn Sook coveted Bel Ahn, but she only had eyes for me. Her scorn enraged Jorn Sook, and he issued false charges of treason against me. I would have stayed and fought, but Bel Ahn discovered Jorn Sook planned to have me executed. She convinced me to flee into exile, saying while I lived she would still have hope. In exile, I fell to brooding and cared not what became of me. It was thus that Kroulk found me, and from thus you have roused me."

I gripped Shom Kerr's shoulder in the universal sign of friendship. "Come with Tars Tarkas and me, Shom Kerr, to the palace of Jorn Sook. There, we will face this tyrant and win back the women we love!"

Shom Kerr's face came alive with fierce determination. As he gripped my shoulder in return, he said, "Yes, John Carter, I will join you! Even should we die in the attempt, we three will give Jorn Sook nightmares to last a lifetime!"

A voice rose from behind Shom Kerr. "You have more than three, Shom Kerr!"

Turning, we beheld forty men, as clean and neat as the conditions allowed, return to the clearing. The man who had spoken stepped forward. "I was a guard in Jorn Sook's palace. He exiled me for helping a servant hide after she had caught Jorn Sook's eye. The palace has many secret passages and entrances, many of which I know. I will cast my lot with you if you will have me, Shom Kerr!"

"Gladly, Trom Jir!" Shom Kerr exclaimed.

Trom Jir turned to his fellows. "Who is with me? Who else will follow where Shom Kerr leads?"

Forty blades flashed into the air as one as every man in the camp cast his lot with Shom Kerr!

I n a land of perpetual light, we could not count on the cover of darkness to hide our movement into the city. This presented little problem to Shom Kerr and his fellow bronze warriors. Slipping me, a white man, into the city unnoticed would be hard enough. Slipping Tars Tarkas in was impossible. Fortune smiled upon us, though.

One of Shom Kerr's men had helped build and maintain Mordon's network of sewers. He volunteered to lead the mighty Thark and me as close to the Jeddak's palace as possible within the sewers. Our guide led us swiftly and safely through the sewers, to within one hundred feet of the palace. The guide climbed out of the sewers and took up a position lounging against a nearby pillar. His presence would let Shom Kerr know

Tars Tarkas and I were in position and waiting. We had not long to wait.

Trom Jir approached the palace and slipped into an alcove in the palace wall. A minute later, he emerged from the alcove and gave a signal. On Trom Jir's signal, five men at the far end of the street began a loud argument that swiftly escalated into a fight. As all attention turned toward the disturbance, Tars Tarkas and I dashed from the sewer toward the alcove. We were in the alcove and through the hidden entrance, Trom Jir had opened before anyone noticed us. Over the next few minutes, Shom Kerr and the rest of his men joined us.

Shom Kerr looked toward Trom Jir. "It's up to you to get us as close to the throne room as possible. I know you will not fail us!"

Trom Jir brought his right fist up and across his chest in salute, then turned to the rest of us. "We are close to the lower kitchens. There are only two guards. The rest are slaves captured from the surface. The slaves will not give us away, but we must kill the guards quickly."

We followed Trom Jir until we heard the sounds of kitchen work ahead. Motioning everyone else to stay back, Shom Kerr and I moved forward for a look into the kitchen. The kitchen was vast and sweltering. Perhaps one hundred red Barsoomians slaved in the kitchen, chained to their posts. Two guards lounged lazily on the far side of the kitchen. An alarm switch was on the wall directly behind them.

"I see but one way to silence the guards, John Carter," Shom Kerr whispered. "The ceiling is high. Can you reach the guards in a single leap?"

In answer, my legs bent, and then I sprang into the room. I judged my leap perfectly, landing directly before the astonished guards. Grabbing one guard by his harness, I threw him as far as my earthly muscles would allow. The second guard tried for the alarm, but my sword thrust made him pull up short. With no other alternative, the guard drew his sword and crossed blades with me.

Apparently, Jorn Sook did not believe kitchen guard duty to be difficult, as the guard would have been no match for many children in Helium. As he dropped to the floor, lifeless, I looked for the second guard. I need not have bothered. My toss had dropped him at the feet of several red men. Using their chains as weapons, they had dispatched the guard quickly and quietly.

"Kaor, John Carter!" one man called out quietly. "I served under your command at—"

"Kaor, Dar Zaan! How could I fail to remember a brave and resourceful warrior such as you?" Taking the guard keys from a hook, I tossed them to Dar Zaan. "There will be time to talk later. For now, free everyone, arm yourselves as best you can, and follow us to the throne room. Today shall mark the end of the Jorn Sook's tyrannical reign in Mordon!"

Trom Jir led us onward. He stopped three times, each time touching a hidden release which opened hidden doorways within the wall. Each time, Shom Kerr sent ten men through the hidden passage, ordering them to reach the throne room and wait for our arrival. Only when Shom Kerr raised his sword were they to attack. Then it was our turn to take a hidden passage. We moved swiftly through the narrow, dusty passage until another door blocked our way.

"This door opens into the entry chamber to Jorn Sook's throne room," Trom Jir said. "Few dare to petition the Jeddak, so we may reach the seneschal without being noticed."

Shom Kerr stepped forward. "You have done well, Trom Jir. From here on, it is my duty to lead."

So saying, he opened the door and stepped out into the chamber. As Trom Jir had suspected, the room was empty. Shom Kerr quickly advanced to the curtains separating this chamber from the throne room. With a quick movement, his hand darted through the curtain and returned clapped over the mouth of a very surprised seneschal! As the rest of us moved to join him, Shom Kerr spoke quietly to the seneschal.

Gaping at him, the seneschal said, "But... But, my lord—"

Placing the point of his sword against the seneschal's back, Shom Kerr said, "Do as I instructed or the Jeddak will need a new seneschal."

Face pale and with a sword at his back, the seneschal stepped back through the curtains. With a loud clap of his hands, the seneschal drew attention to himself, yet said nothing.

A lazy voice from within the throne room said, "Well, seneschal? I believe this is where you announce those who come to petition me."

Mocking laughter rose from the nobles in the throne room.

"Y-yes, my J-Jeddak," the seneschal stammered. "Jorn Sook, J-Jeddak of M-Mordon, ruler of Barsoom both above and below, v-visitors beg an audience with you!"

"More fool them," the same lazy voice said, causing more laughter to ripple through the throne room.

This time, the seneschal controlled his fear. Speaking in a loud, clear voice, he said, "May it please the court, I announce Shom Kerr, noble of Mordon, Tars Tarkas, Jeddak of Thark and John Carter, Prince of Helium and Warlord of Barsoom!"

The mocking laughter cut off as Shom Kerr, Tars Tarkas and I swept into the throne room, ten of our men at our heels. As we passed in, the seneschal turned and ran from the hall. All around the entry to the throne room, nobles and sycophants backed away from us. Across the room, the throne sat upon a dais. The man sitting upon it stared at us as if we were spirits returned from the dead. At his feet, chains around their necks, sat two women. The beautiful woman on the left only had eyes for Shom Kerr. Knowing this must be Bel Ahn, I looked at the other woman and gazed right into the eyes of my incomparable Dejah Thoris!

Even as both women reached toward Shom Kerr and me, Jorn Sook called out, "Guards! Take those men into custody!"

Dozens of guards ran out from all corners, surrounding our small band. Swords leveled, they advanced warily upon us. Then Shom Kerr raised his sword. Three hidden doors flew open and, with savage cries, the rest of our men poured into the room! The court sycophants cowered and hid. The few nobles present drew their swords but were unsure whom to fight.

As Tars Tarkas and I fought back to back, my sword weaving a net of steel before me, I called out over the din of battle, "Nobles of Mordon, if you would have a tyrant for jeddak, join the attack against us. But if you would have a fair and just jeddak, if you would be free men, join us, and we will bring down the tyrant Jorn Sook!"

All doubt fled from the eyes of the nobles. As one they joined the fray, calling, "Death to Jorn Sook! Death to the tyrant!"

The battle ranged across the throne room, with neither side gaining the upper hand. In disgust, I noticed Jorn Sook never once drew the sword he wore at his side. Instead, he stayed on his throne, eying the battle with the intensity of a man who knows his life hangs in the balance. Then the red men from the kitchen charged into the throne room, and the tide of the battle turned swiftly for us!

Seeing this, Jorn Sook quailed. He touched a panel on his throne and yet another hidden door opened, this one behind his throne. Grasping the chain around Dejah Thoris's neck, Jorn Sook began pulling my beloved toward the door. Immediately, Bel Ahn leaped to her aid, pulling back on the chain so it was no longer choking her. Jorn Sook backhanded Bel Ahn hard, sending her tumbling down the dais. No longer burdened by the weight of both women, Jorn Sook slowly dragged Dejas Thoris toward the hidden door!

Even as I watched this, my blade flashed before me. Chance brought the moment I was waiting for. My blade flashed at a wrist holding a raised sword. The sword, with the guard's hand still gripping it, dropped neatly into my left hand. With a flick of my wrist, I sent the sword spinning over the battle and towards the dais.

"Bel Ahn! Dejah Thoris!" I called. "The sword! Get the sword!"

Both women heard me, as did Jorn Sook. As the sword landed on the floor and slid toward the dais, Dejas Thoris lunged toward the blade. At the same moment, Jorn Sook hauled viciously on the chain and the sword slid just beyond her reach! But it slid right into the hands of Bel Ahn. Showing herself a true daughter of Barsoom, Bel Ahn ignored the severed hand as she swung the blade around toward Jorn Sook. With a cry of feminine fury, she drove the sword straight through the Jeddak of Mordon!

Wrenching it free, Bel Ahn held the bloody blade above her head and called out, "Behold! Jorn Sook, tyrant of Mordon, is dead!"

The fighting stopped as all heads turned toward the dais. They saw Bel Ahn, sword still held triumphant, help Dejah Thoris to her feet. Taking advantage of the moment, I leaped over all to land next to the two women.

"Men of Mordon," I said, "your jeddak lies dead, slain while attempting to flee the battle! Is this the kind of man you want as your jeddak?"

Shom Kerr and his men all shouted, "No!"

"Would you have a jeddak who is brave and noble?" I asked. "A jeddak who will guarantee freedom, not oppression?"

"Yes!" our men shouted, this time joined by the nobles and a few of the guards.

"The man you want is here!" I said. "He is Shom Kerr! What say you men of Mordon? What say you to Shom Kerr, Jeddak of Mordon?"

The blades of Shom Kerr's men flashed aloft, followed almost immediately by those of the nobles and many of the guards. Over the next few seconds, all swords rose to support Shom Kerr.

"All hail Shom Kerr, Jeddak of Mordon!" rang one hundred voices.

In the days that followed, the temporary tunnel connected Mordon and Helium yet again. The nations exchanged diplomatic courtesies, negotiated treaties and trade deals, and made plans for permanent tunnels linking the Mordon with the surface of Barsoom. But these are not tasks for a man of action. Dejah Thoris and I stayed for Shom Kerr's coronation and his marriage to Bel Ahn. Then, with my arm around the incomparable Dejah Thoris, we traversed the long tunnel home.

DARKNESS FALLS

Working the biplane's controls with the practiced ease only possible from a former flying ace, Cliff Hanger pointed to the hilltop farm ahead.

"Cote? Are you sure that's the place?" Cliff yelled over the roar of the aeroplane's engine.

Cliff's younger brother struggled to keep the map open against the buffeting wind and yelled back, "If what Beth said over the telephone before they cut her off is correct, then that's the place!"

Giving Cote a thumbs up signal, Cliff was about to turn back toward the hill when he saw the other aircraft. Swooping down out of the sun and the clouds came half a dozen black-painted aeroplanes. Minions of the evil Doctor Darkness

As he went into a barrel roll, Cliff hollered, "Doctor Darkness has sent us an unwelcoming party. Hang on, little brother!"

Machine guns chattered from the pursuing aeroplanes as Cliff dived, climbed and rolled, putting on such a flying exhibition as he hadn't attempted since he last flew his Spad on combat missions during the Great War. But back then, he had machine guns of his own and could take the fight to the enemy. Now, he could only play this airborne game of dodge-ball and hope to reach the farm before one of the dark doctor's minions got lucky. Even as that thought flitted through his mind, the gods of chance turned against Cliff. A stream of bullets stitched the little aeroplane's fuselage, and the last one plowed into the engine!

On the hilltop below, Beth Key, plucky reporter for the Denver Sentinel, cried out in dismay as black smoke sprouted from Cliff's aeroplane. At the same moment, it began rapidly losing altitude.

"Bwa ha ha ha ha ha!" crowed Doctor Darkness. "So much for the Hanger boys! Your precious Cliff and his little brother Cote are doomed! Doomed! Now nothing stands between me and the power I deserve!" Looking directly into Beth's eyes, Doctor Darkness added, "And the woman I desire!"

Struggling in the evil man's steely grip, Beth declared, "My heart belongs to Cliff, and it will for as long as he lives!"

Turning back to the plummeting aeroplane, Doctor Darkness said, "Which should not be very much longer, Miss Key. Not much longer at all!"

Even as he spoke, the little aeroplane seemed to pull out of its dive, leveling off. Beth's hopes lifted as Cliff fought to land the mortally wounded craft. But just as it looked as if Cliff had the aeroplane under control, skimming the ground at terrible speed, it flew into the farm's big, abandoned barn. Seconds later, an explosion rocked the hilltop, and the barn burst into flames!

Beth stared at the burning barn in stunned horror as Doctor Darkness cackled beside her. Beth cried, "You evil fiend!"

"Now, my dear Beth," the dastardly doctor said, "is that any way to talk to your husband-to-be?"

Doctor Darkness grabbed Beth and pulled her into his arms. His lascivious lips pressed against hers. The revolted reporter kicked Doctor Darkness in the shins, following it with a round-house right to the jaw.

"Keep your pathetic paws off of me!" Beth cried, raising her fists and taking a pugilist's stance.

"Foolish female, your fists have sealed your fate! It's the Mind Manipulator for you," spat Doctor Darkness. "You'll be quite my willing and eager slave in a matter of minutes!"

Seeing two of his minions approaching, the leering leader waved them over. "Take Miss Key to the airship and prepare her for a mental maladjustment!"

Crack! Doctor Darkness reeled from the punch of one of his minions.

"Did you notice how I drove through the punch, Beth?" a familiar voice asked. "You still need to work on that!"

"Cliff!" Beth cried, her face lighting up with joy as she threw her arms around him.

"Curse you, Hanger!" Doctor Darkness said, struggling to his feet. "You should be dead!"

Cote Hanger stepped up next to his brother, picking hay from his hair. "Then you shouldn't leave piles of hay in your abandoned barns, Doctor Dumbness! Jumping into the hay was a piece of cake compared to stunts we did in during our barnstorming days!"

Sensing a great ending to the story she would write for her newspaper, Beth pulled out her notebook and pencil. Stepping toward Doctor Darkness, she asked, "Once again, the Hanger brothers have foiled your nefarious plans, Doctor Darkness. Do you have any last words before they take you to jail?"

"Yes, Miss Key, I do. Always have an ace up your sleeve. An ace reporter, that is!" The devious doctor grabbed Beth, pulled a snub-nosed revolver from his pocket, and put it to the lovely lady's head. "Back off, Hanger boys, or the ace reporter will be an ex-reporter!"

Knowing Beth's life hung in the balance, Cliff backed away. "This isn't over, you malicious miscreant! I'll pursue you to the ends of the earth to save Beth!"

Backing into the farmhouse, Doctor Darkness laughed. "You deluded dolt! One minute under my Mind Manipulator and Miss Key will forget all about you!"

The farmhouse door slammed shut, cutting off Beth's protests.

"Now what, Cliff?" asked Cote.

"Evil doesn't have a long attention span," Cliff said. "Give it a count of five, Cote, then we hit the door."

Cliff held his hand up, counting down on his fingers. At zero, the brothers lowered their shoulders and charged into the door. Unable to stand against their righteousness might, the door crashed open! The brothers sped through the little house. But the evil man and his beautiful hostage were gone!

"Golly, Cliff, they can't have just disappeared!" Cote exclaimed.

"Look for a trapdoor," Cliff ordered. "Doctor Darkness must have a lair inside the hill!"

At that moment, both men tumbled from their feet as the farm house shook, rumbled, and began tilting to one side. As Cliff slid toward one wall, his hands scrabbled to find something to cling to. His fingertips caught on something poking out in the middle of the floor. It was the trapdoor!

As he pulled the hidden hatch open, Cliff called. "Cote! Can you reach my foot and climb up here? I've got a feeling we have to get through this door or I will lose Beth forever!"

Cote, an experienced climber, soon joined his brother at the opening in the floor. The two men gaped at the sight before them. The roar of powerful engines rattled the house. It was a huge aeroplane, with its wings and the eight engines mounted on the wings rotated to face up. The mammoth craft was slowly lifting straight up!

Cliff shook off his admiration of the amazing aeroplane, reminding himself that Beth was counting on him. "Come on, little brother. We've got an aeroplane to catch!"

So saying, Cliff pulled himself up onto the now-vertical lip of the trapdoor, then launched himself at the rising aeroplane's horizontal stabilizer. Landing in a crouch, Cliff steadied himself by grabbing the vertical stabilizer. With a thump, Cote landed next to him.

"We've got to get to the cockpit!" Cliff had to yell to be heard over the engines.

Cote nodded and the two brothers set off across the curving fuselage. Cliff silently thanked the Lord for the years they spent wing walking in the aerial show owned and operated by Beth's father. Without that experience, they'd surely plummet to their deaths! Instead, mere moments passed before they stood above the rear cargo hatch.

The stronger of the two, Cliff braced himself, and lowered his brother head first toward the hatch. Only the narrowness of the tapering fuselage made it possible for Cote to reach the handle, but reach it, he did! Seconds later, the two determined men stood safely inside the aeroplane.

"It's time we gave Doctor Darkness the what for!" Cliff said, striding purposefully toward the cockpit.

"Dang right, big brother!" Cote said, pounding his fist into palm. "Dang right."

Cliff pushed through the hatch from the cargo compartment and into the vast passenger compartment. Expecting row after row of seats, Cliff was again surprised at the dastardly doctor's inventiveness. Strange machinery lined the walls, colorful lights flashed, levers and knobs protruded from nearly every surface, and the whir of spinning gears filled the compartment.

Astounding as the sight was, Cliff's eyes were drawn inexorably to the front of the aeroplane, where Beth struggled futilely as Doctor Darkness strapped her into a chair. Wires ran from the machinery to the chair and then to an ominous metal helmet that hung above Beth's head.

Cliff sprang forward like a sprinter coming out of the starting blocks! At the sound of pounding feet, Doctor Darkness spun around and raised his snub-nosed revolver. Beth's hands were strapped to the chair arms, but her feet were still free. Seeing the foul villain drawing a bead on the man she loved, Beth kicked him in the back of the knee.

Doctor Darkness's knee buckled, and his shot went wide. He never had time to take a second shot, as Cliff's haymaker lifted the emissary of evil off his feet and sent him flying backward! Cote arrived just in time to kick the revolver away from the doctor's reaching hand.

Doctor Darkness scrambled away from the Hanger brothers. "No! How can simpletons such as the two of you foil my brilliant plans?"

"It's simple—good always triumphs over evil!" Cliff said as he removed the straps holding Beth to the chair.

"This is no triumph for you, Hanger," Doctor Darkness snarled. "Merely a setback for me!"

With that, the doctor snatched a parachute hanging nearby and wrenched open the forward hatch. Looking over his shoulder, the doctor said, "You will be mine, Beth Key! So swears Doctor Darkness!"

"Don't jump!" Cliff cried.

But the warning came too late. With the wings rotated vertically, the maniacal mastermind leaped into the nearest propellor! Beth buried her head into Cliff's chest as bits of Doctor Darkness splattered against the outer fuselage.

"Yuck!" Cote said as he shut the forward hatch. "That guy goes all to pieces when loses."

Chuckling at his own joke, Cote looked into the cockpit. "Hey Cliff, there's some kind of machine up here, and it's flying this aeroplane!"

When Cliff didn't reply, Cote looked back. Beth had her arms wrapped around Cliff's neck and was kissing Cliff soundly. To Cote's eye, Cliff looked to be giving as good as he got.

"I'll just figure out how to fly this thing on my own, okay?" When no answer came, Cote smiled and made his way to the cockpit. "Thought so."

THE GIFT

I cannot walk on water. I cannot raise the dead. I cannot feed a multitude with a few loaves and fishes. I am not the second coming of the Christ, though there are those who believe I am because of what I *can* do.

I can cure the sick. I can let the blind see. I can make the crippled walk.

It is my gift.

It is my curse.

Jane and I were in Africa, though I forget which country. I can never keep them straight, anyway. We'd been in the village for four days. One more day should be enough to complete the healing. One more day and then it was on to the next village and its people and their wretched conditions.

I was cleaning up after the day's work when I saw the cloud of dust from an approaching truck. In this village, trucks inspire fear. Rarely, they bring supplies or people like me who only wish to help the villagers. More often they bring a warlord's thugs or, worse, soldiers from the government.

The villagers gathered their children and hid in their huts. Jane and I went to our hut as well. While Jane checked her guns, I watched the approaching truck.

"Here," Jane said, tossing me a pistol. "Turn the safety off."

I flicked the safety off and shoved the gun into my pants pocket. Jane never trusts me to remember basic gun safety. "I do know how to handle a gun, dear."

"If by 'handle' you mean 'shoot yourself', then I guess you do," she replied.

I shrugged. "I can't shoot well enough to hit anyone else."

The truck stopped in the village center, and five heavily armed men jumped out. One fired two shots into the air.

"We come for the healer!" he shouted. "We know he is here. Bring him to us!"

"Stay here and cover me," I said to Jane and then walked out the door.

Five guns covered me as I approached. The one who called for me kept talking, but I ignored him. I'd been through this routine in other villages and knew what was coming. The script never changes. There was a gun battle. The warlord was badly wounded. He would only survive if I healed him. His men threaten the villagers, who will pay with their lives if I fail. Yada yada yada. Yes, I knew this scene all too well.

But I was wrong.

Blankets had been piled in the back of the truck, forming a kind of nest. A woman was curled up in the nest, holding a newborn child. The woman's breath came fast and sweat covered her face. Anyone could see she was dying. The infant wasn't doing well, either. The child rasped and wheezed, fighting for breath. A large, powerful man—the local warlord—cradled the woman's head in his lap.

He looked at me, his eyes shining, and said, "Healer, you must help my wife and my son! You must heal them! If you do not, my men will raze this vil—"

Climbing into the back of the truck, I said, "Stop making threats. If you know enough to bring your family here, you know I will help them."

I gave the woman an encouraging smile and gestured toward

the baby. She held him out to me. As soon as I touched him, I knew the child's problem. His lungs had not fully cleared, and he was slowly suffocating. It took but a thought, and the boy's lungs cleared. My lungs, from the same thought, filled. As the boy let out his first cry, my gift cleared my lungs before I even coughed.

Placing the boy back in his mother's arms, I took her hand and sensed internal bleeding. Without immediate help, she would be dead in minutes. Back when Jane and I still lived in the States, I'd have had no idea how to treat the mother. Her uterus was the source of the bleeding. I couldn't simply transfer her wound to me and let my gift heal it, for no man has a uterus. But injuries like this are all too common in Africa. I've long since learned to work around our bodies' differences. I must concentrate harder to transfer the wound elsewhere—my stomach, I decided—but I can do it. Perspiration beaded on my forehead as I worked. A minute later, her bleeding stopped. A few seconds after that, my gift sealed the rip I had moved into my stomach.

"The boy is healthy now. Feed him and he'll be fine," I told the warlord. "Your wife will need to rest for several days, but she'll recover as well. She may feed the child, but someone should handle everything else until her strength returns."

I stood and climbed from the truck, leaving the warlord staring at his wife and child in wonder.

"So, the stories are true," he said. "You truly are a magic man."

"No magic, but yes," I replied, turning back to my hut, "the stories are true."

"I thank you for the lives of my family," the warlord said, "but I cannot let a man of your value leave. From now on you work for me, healer."

Damn, we were back on script again. Why can't men like this warlord simply leave me in peace? Reaching into my pocket, I gripped the pistol. I even remembered to check the safety. It was still off.

"You're hardly the first man to try holding me," I said. "You won't have any more success than those who tried before you. Your wife and son will live. Rejoice in that knowledge and leave while you still can."

"Hold him," the warlord barked. Laughing without humor, he added, "You are a healer, not a warrior. You will do as I say."

Two of the warlord's men grabbed my arms and pulled me toward the truck. Dammit, I *hate* hurting people, but idiots like the warlord leave me no choice. Gritting my teeth, I pulled the trigger of the pistol in my pocket. Pain flared as the bullet blasted into and through my thigh, cutting my femoral artery. I pushed away the pain just as I pushed away the wound. The man on my right screamed in agony and dropped to the ground. Blood fountained from the fresh wound in his leg.

My gift to him.

From behind me, I heard the crack of Jane's rifle and a man near the truck dropped. The man holding my left arm looked at his bleeding companion with incomprehension. Tightening his grip on my arm, he hurried toward the truck. I fired the pistol into my leg a second time. The man fell screaming as blood spurted from his leg.

My gift to him.

Jane fired twice more, and the warlord's last two men went down, already dead or bleeding to death from my gifts. The warlord's head swung back and forth, shock and confusion contorting his face..

"You can still take your family and leave," I told him, praying he would act reasonably.

Anger washed over the man's face, and he leapt from the truck. "You will heal my men! You will come with me!"

The fool still thought he could win. Yet, by leaving the truck, he made himself an easier target. Jane could shoot at him without worrying about hitting the woman or child. This warlord was quicker than I expected though. He grabbed me, spun around to face my hut, and pointed a pistol at my head.

"Stop shooting!" he yelled. "Stop shooting or I will kill the healer!"

"You're already a dead man," I told him, "you just haven't fallen down yet."

I heard the crack of Jane's rifle and felt the bullet pierce my chest. It tore through me and into the warlord. Without conscious thought, I passed my wound to the warlord.

My gift to him.

The arm around my throat went slack, and the warlord dropped to the ground. As the light faded from his eyes, I yelled, "Dammit, all you had to do was leave! Why don't people like you *ever* leave? Why do you always make me kill you?"

Turning back to the truck, I found the warlord's wife was staring at me, her eyes wide and terrified.

"I did not want to orphan your son on his birthday," I told her, "but his father gave me no choice. Don't worry, I do not blame you for his actions."

"W-what will h-happen to me?" she asked through trembling lips.

"Someone from the village will drive you home. You will tell your husband's men what happened here. They will give the villagers the truck and let them return home safely. The men will leave this village alone or they will face my wrath. Do you understand?"

Her head bobbed up and down rapidly.

The warlord's men would obey my commands. They always do. Superstition is still a powerful force in rural Africa. Fear of my gift would keep them in line.

Though my gift means life for the wretched, it is death for the wicked.

TRANSPORTED

We were in the middle of our second set when the warning came. I broke off mid-song and called into the mike, "Fed alert! Fed alert!"

Some of the first timers in the audience panicked, but veteran concert goers quickly took them under their wings. The guys and I had been through the drill so many times that our moves were as well rehearsed as the songs we'd been playing. Abandoning our equipment, we slipped through our back stage bolt hole and down into the city's abandoned sewers. While we ran, we could hear sounds coming from other tunnels as our fans used the same escape route.

The old sewers are always safe. No one in the Federation uses anything as primitive as sewers anymore; not when there are so many *cleaner* options. And the sewers were really dirty. No Fed is ever willing to get his hands dirty just to track down an underground rock band and their fans.

So we ran and our fans ran and the only thing the Feds found were the instruments we'd left behind. When we came to our exit from the tunnels, a quick tricorder reading showed no one waiting on the street above. We climbed out of the sewer and split up, each of us heading for a different transporter station.

Minutes later, I transported to within a short walk from my house. One nice thing about transporters, you can set them to clean your clothes in transit. Mom and Dad didn't even suspect a thing when I walked into the house.

I volunteered to replicate dinner that night. Not only does it always please my parents, it also gave me a chance to check the replication mass balance. An electric guitar takes a lot of mass to replicate, and I have to work carefully to save enough mass so it goes unnoticed. I make a lot of pasta for that reason. I replicate uncooked pasta and then cook it in boiling water. It's so 21st century, but I save a lot of mass going that route. Another couple of my pasta dinners and I'd be back in business.

Over dinner, Mom brought up the concert. "I heard Security broke up another one of those illicit rock and roll concerts up in New Seattle today."

"Did they catch anybody?" I asked, trying to be casual.

"No, all the little hooligans got away," she answered.

"Aren't you being a bit harsh on them, dear?" Dad asked. "They're probably just kids acting out a bit. Rebelling against authority and all that. History is full of examples—"

Mom interrupted, "History is full of war and disease and famine, too, Tom. Does that mean the Federation was wrong to eliminate those?"

"Now, Alice," Dad said, "don't get all worked up. There's a big difference between some teenagers trying to thumb their noses at the Security forces and war."

"Really? Didn't you pay attention in history, Tom?" Mom asked, getting worked up. "The rise of that awful rock and roll music led directly to the global disasters of the 21st century! How can you—"

"Mom, Dad, can't we have a fun, argument free dinner tonight?" I asked.

Dad, calm as ever, said, "Sure thing, buddy."

Mom worked hard to put a smile on her face. "Of course,

dear. At least I can be confident *you* weren't one of those teens in New Seattle listening to that trash!"

"Guaranteed, Mom," I said. "I'd never be in the audience at a rock and roll show!"

'I'd be in front of the audience playing the music,' went unsaid.

"Of course not, Jeff," Mom said. "The youngest first chair violin in the history of the San Francisco Youth Orchestra is far too talented to be interested in that sort of garbage."

Before anyone could say anything else, the door chimed. With an '*I wonder who that could be*' look, Mom got up to answer the door. I heard the murmur of voices, then Mom came back to the dining room. She looked pale and angry. Behind her was a Security officer. He carried my guitar.

"Jeff," Mom said, her voice strained, "this gentleman has some questions to ask you."

The Security officer stepped forward, holding up my guitar. "We picked this up at an illegal rock and roll show up in New Seattle. We believe the leader of a band that calls itself Seedy Underbelly abandoned it. Would you know anything about that?"

Okay, this wasn't good, but it wasn't the end of the world, either. We all wore Second Skin on any part of our bodies that would touch our instruments. No bio material for Security to use to track us down. I don't know how he still traced me, but he wouldn't have any actual proof.

"Why would I know anything about this, sir?" I asked, going into my Federation-approved polite young man act.

"Because you are the leader of this so-called band," the officer replied. "Oh, you've been a very careful boy, I'll admit. I'm guessing you use Second Skin while you're playing. But even the most careful criminal eventually makes a mistake. Today was your day to make that mistake."

Continuing with the polite youngster act, I said, "I'm afraid I have no idea what you're talking about, sir."

The Security officer smiled at me. It was not reassuring.

"Today, when you dropped this guitar and fled from our raid, the guitar nicked you where you didn't have any Second Skin. I'm guessing your leg, but it really doesn't matter. We picked up solid bio evidence from this instrument."

"Oh," I said, numbly.

"Jeff," Mom said, her voice rising, "I'm sure there's a perfectly good explanation why your DNA was on this guitar. Tell him!"

"What can I tell him, Mom?" I asked. "He's right. He's got me."

I'll save you the scene that followed. Mom went for histrionics. Dad went for calm, but in such a sad, almost depressed, way that I wished he would have gotten mad or something. It was almost a relief when the Security officer led me away.

The trial was both boring and virtually non-existent. With the DNA evidence, my conviction was a forgone conclusion. They kept badgering me to tell them who else was in the band. The Feds threatened me with worse punishment if I didn't tell. They offered me reduced punishment if I told on my bandmates. At their lowest, they sent Mom and Dad in to 'try to talk sense' into me. It was the night of my arrest all over again, only a hundred times worse. None of their threats or tricks had any effect. Regardless of what happened, my days as a rock and roller were over. There was nothing they could possibly do that was worse than that.

At the sentencing, I learned just how wrong I was.

"Jeff Morrow," the judge intoned from his bench, "you have been found guilty of forming, playing in, and leading an illegal rock and roll band. You have refused to cooperate in any way with the prosecution. Therefore, I have no choice but to give you the maximum sentence."

Behind me, Mom gasped. I didn't know what the judge was talking about.

"You are hereby sentenced to be transported," the judge

continued. "The sentence is to be carried out immediately. Have you anything to say?"

"I don't understand the sentence," I said. "What does being transported mean?"

"It means, young man," the judge leaned toward me, "you will soon be a happy and productive citizen of the Federation!"

I still had no idea what was going on. Mom quietly cried on Dad's shoulder as Security led me out of the courtroom. We went to a room just down the hall from the courtroom. There was a transporter in the room, but not like one I'd ever seen before. This one had five Security techs at the controls and just a single transport plate. They led me directly to the plate. A force field quickly formed around me, keeping me from stepping off of it.

"What's going on?" I shouted, banging on the force field.

No one paid any attention to me. One of the techs ran his hands across the controls and I felt a tingle.

"Readings acquired," the tech said. He looked at the other four techs. "Awaiting modification parameters."

The other techs bent over their controls for a minute. When the last of the techs sat back, the first tech announced, "All modification parameters are set. Prepare for transporting."

A low hum filled the room as the transporter came online. I still didn't know what was happening, but whatever it was scared the crap out of me.

I banged on the force field again. "Stop! Let me out of here! All I did was play some music!"

No one even looked up. Suddenly, the transporter beam engulfed me. Somehow, it felt different from other transporter beams. No, I felt different within this beam. I felt parts of myself going away. I felt—

The transporter stopped, and the force field dropped away. A smiling tech helped me down off the platform.

"How are you feeling, Jeff?" he asked.

"Hm? Oh, fine, thank you, sir," I replied. Then I noticed the clock. "Is that the time? I'm going to be late for orchestra rehearsal!"

"Don't worry, Jeff," the tech said, "this Security officer will take you directly to a public transporter platform. You'll be there in no time!"

The officer stepped forward and held something out toward me. "I believe this is yours, Jeff."

I gave it a quick glance. "A guitar? I've never played one, sir. I'm a violinist."

He smiled, put the guitar aside, and said, "My mistake, Jeff. Now, let's get you to that transporter station."

I made it to rehearsal just in time.

THE NOMOD

"D r. Tanner, we've got the nomod for you," the Guard said, poking his head through the office door.

"Thank you, uh..." I cast around, trying to remember the Guard's name and couldn't. "He's been scanned for diseases and parasites?"

"Yep. Came up clean as a whistle."

I squashed a surge of irritation at the cliché. You can't really expect anything more from a Guard, after all. "Show him in, please."

The Guard led a young man into my office. The nomod looked to be in his mid-twenties, perhaps a bit older. He was tall, nearly as tall as the Guard, though not so heavily muscled. I gestured to a chair opposite my desk.

"Want me to stay, Doc?" asked the Guard. "In case he gets any ideas?"

"No, I'm sure there won't be any problems." I looked at the nomod, "You're not going to get any ideas, are you?"

The nomod laughed, "I've got plenty of ideas already, but I expect I'll be getting some new ones, too. That's why you're so scared of nomods, after all."

The Guard scowled and shook the nomod roughly. "You

show some respect for the Doc, nomod, or you're going to answer to me and my five friends."

The Guard slowly, dramatically closed the fingers of his right hand into a fist.

"That's enough, Guard," I said sharply. "You may wait outside the office. I'll call should this man get any of your ideas."

The Guard let go of the nomod. "I'll be watching you!"

Looking at me, the nomod said, "Through a closed door? I'm very impressed, Tanner. Fifty years into the mods program and you've already developed x-ray vision!"

The Guard looked at me, puzzled. I smiled and waved him toward the door. "That will be all, Guard. Please close the door on your way out."

As the door closed, the nomod said, "I don't think he missed a single one of the standard guard phrases. Is there a special class that teaches Guards how to talk like that?"

"Due to their intellectual limits, much of their early training involves watching guards in old movies and television shows. They can more easily absorb what it means to be a Guard through video. Unfortunately, many of those same videos feature the unimaginative dialogue you just heard." I looked the nomod in the eyes. "But that's not why we're here."

As if he hadn't heard me, the nomod stared straight into my eyes. "Does it make you proud? Knowing what has been done to him and all the other Guards?"

"What on earth do you mean?" I asked, though I know well what he meant.

"What kind of life is that for a person?" he said. "Limited intellect, no curiosity, nothing to do but stand around and spout trite phrases."

Just as I suspected. I smiled. "He's quite content with his lot in life and wouldn't trade it for any other. You can ask him yourself if you don't believe me."

"Of course he wouldn't trade it," scoffed the nomod. "You modded everything out of him that didn't fit the narrow definition of Guard. He not only doesn't know there's anything else to life, he *can't* know!"

I nodded, "That's correct. Are you suggesting there is something wrong with that?"

"Of course there is!" the nomod shouted. "That Guard had no choice in his own future. The decisions were made for him in a mod lab before he was born!"

The door opened, and the Guard looked in. "He getting wise with you, Doc?"

"He's a little excited, that's all," I replied. "Thank you for your concern."

"Just doing my job, Doc." The Guard smiled and shut the door.

"There, you see? He's quite happy with his life. You seem to think we are monsters when all we did was create contentment, leveling the playing field for everyone."

"Leveling the playing field? A level playing field implies some kind of competition," the nomod said. "You canceled the game completely! But that's not the worst of it. By meddling, you're destroying mankind."

"That's a tad melodramatic, don't you think?" I asked.

The nomod didn't answer. He was looking out the window, captivated by something. All I could see was a group of children quietly riding their bicycles to the nearby school. Suddenly, the nomod stood up. Slightly alarmed, I was about to call the Guard when he spoke.

"Let's go out and talk to those kids for a few minutes." Noticing the alarm on my face, he added, "You can bring your pet Guard and have him kick my ass if I do anything out of line."

I hesitated, trying to figure out what the nomod was planning.

"I'm not going to do anything to them," he said. "Just ask them a few questions. You and the goon will be right there. What are you scared of?"

I must admit, he had piqued my curiosity. I nodded, and we left the office.

The children had just parked their bikes as we approached. I knew the group, as I did all the Science children in the center. "Hello children," I said.

"Hello Dr. Tanner," two dozen voices said in unison.

"Spooky," said the nomod, drawing the children's attention for the first time.

"Children, this man would like to ask you a few questions," I told them.

"I saw all of you riding down the road a few minutes ago," the nomod said. "Do you like riding your bikes?"

The children milled about, looking at one another and then back to the nomod. No one spoke. The nomod rolled his eyes.

"You," he said, pointing to the boy closest to him. "Do you like riding your bike?"

"It's an efficient form of transportation for short distances," the boy answered.

"But do you *like* it?" the nomod persisted.

"I don't understand the question," the boy said.

"And you were all riding so... So politely," the nomod continued. "Didn't any of you want to race each other to the bike rack?"

The boy looked puzzled. "Why would we want to race?"

"Because it's fun!" said the nomod.

"We're Science caste," the boy said, "not Athlete caste. Perhaps you should direct your question to one of them."

"Okay, enough about bikes," the nomod said. "How old are you?"

Relieved to be back in known territory, the boy answered, "Thirteen years, four months, eleven days and—"

"That's good enough. No need to calculate it down to the second," the nomod interrupted. He lowered his voice somewhat, "Thirteen, huh? That's about the age I discovered girls.

What about you? Is there a girl in your class that you particularly like?"

"I don't understand your question," the boy said.

"If you're embarrassed, you can come up and speak quietly, just to me," the nomod told him.

"I am not embarrassed," the boy told him. "I don't understand the question."

The nomod pointed to a girl in the class. "What about her? Don't you think she's pretty?"

The boy looked, "Her features are quite symmetrical. Is that what you mean?"

The nomod sighed and turned back to me. "That's enough. Let's go back to your office."

"Very well," I said. "Children, please go on to class."

"Yes, Dr. Tanner," they all said in unison.

Back in the office, the nomod slumped in the chair, looking dejected. "It's worse than even I thought."

"What's worse?" I asked.

"Tanner, you're a premod, right?" he asked. "Born before all the embryonic research, the gene splicing, the literal construction of people, from the ground up, to perform specific tasks?"

"I'm hardly a nomod," I said, "but, yes, I am a premod. I was about the age of those children when the modifications began. I received several post-birth mods, all of which focused and honed my natural abilities."

"But you remember being thirteen?" he asked.

"Of course I do."

"When I was thirteen," the nomod continued, "I had an absolute crush on this nomod girl named Jan. She was tall and slender, with long blond hair and green eyes. I thought she was the most beautiful girl on earth, but I couldn't even work up the nerve to speak to her. What about you, Tanner? Who was your crush when you were thirteen?"

"Penny," I said, without even thinking. "She was such a pretty girl, a cheerleader on the middle school squad. Unlike you, I worked up the nerve to speak to Penny. She was really a very sweet girl, letting me down so softly she almost made it seem as it was her loss that she wouldn't go out with me."

"What about that boy I spoke with?" the nomod asked. "Doesn't he deserve to have a crush on a girl? He'll never waste an afternoon just dreaming about kissing a pretty girl for the first time. Hell, he'll never have dreams!"

"Thirteen used to be a very awkward and painful age," I retorted. "Would you really wish that upon those children?"

"Do I wish they had actual human emotions, you mean?" the nomod shot back. "If that's the question, then yes, I do wish that."

"And yet you sit there thinking I am the monster," I said. "As with the Guard, the children are—"

"Content," he interrupted. "Yeah, oh so content. But you know what, Tanner? Human progress comes from discontent."

"Oh please," I said, an edge of irritation creeping into my voice. "You're just a typical malcontent who wants everyone else to be as miserable as you are!"

"That computer on your desk, Tanner," the nomod said. "It's brand new, right? Cutting edge processing speed, top of the line everything?"

The sudden shift of subject had me at a loss for a moment. "Uh... I... I don't know. What does that have to do—"

"I know the model, trust me. Did you know that computer is twice as fast as the fastest desktop model available thirty years ago, when your first generation of modified people started taking over the jobs nomod humans used to do?"

"Well, no," I said, "but that just serves to disprove your point. Those modified people you denigrate *are* making progress!"

"Ha! I guess computer hardware really isn't your field, is it?" he said.

"So?" I asked, testily.

"So, back in the premod days when poor, discontented

nomods were all the human race had, computer processing speed doubled every two or three years," he said. "Look up Moore's Law sometime, if you don't believe me. In the thirty years your wonderful, contented modified humans have been on the job, computer processing power has only doubled once. Doesn't that tell you something?"

This surprised me, but kept it from my face and voice. "No, it doesn't. I'm certain some physical limitation is responsible for slowing down our progress."

The nomod leaned back in his chair, looking up at the ceiling. "Everyone in the nomod settlement told me not to bother trying to convince you. I guess I should have listened."

"What do you mean?" I asked.

"Look, Tanner, I didn't come here to argue genetics," he said.

"Come here?" I laughed. "No, you didn't come here. You were captured and brought here!"

"Nope. I allowed myself to be captured so I could deliver a message to you," the nomod said. "The message is simple. There are a lot more of us nomods than you think, and we aren't going to take it anymore. We're tired of watching you and your kind destroy the human race. So we're going to put a stop to it."

"That's preposterous! How dare you—"

"That's only part of the message," the nomod interrupted. "We will do our best to minimize casualties, so when you receive an evacuation warning from us, please heed the warning and evacuate everyone. We will provide ample warning for an orderly evacuation of any building or complex targeted."

"Guard!" I called out.

The Guard sprang through the door as if he had been waiting all his life for this call. I suppose he had. "I'm finished interrogating the nomod for today. Take him to his holding cell."

As the Guard led the nomod away, I said, "I'll speak more with you tomorrow."

The nomod smiled, "No, you won't."

He was right. The next morning, Guards found his holding cell empty except for a note. They brought the note to me.

It takes imagination to be a guard. You've got to be able to think as a prisoner would think. Too bad you modded imagination out of your Guards—and everyone else. Don't forget—heed our warnings!

The first of those warnings came two weeks later. The nomods were good to their word, always allowing enough time to evacuate facilities. Despite the nomods' continued success at destroying facilities, their actions were never more than irritants. They certainly never came close to bringing the world to its knees.

It took us years to realize the attacks had merely been diversions. While we tried to stop their attacks, they compromised the embryonic modification computers. Nomods took over the entire mod process without our knowledge. It took us years to realize what they had done. Even then, we only realized it as those nomod children failed to follow what should have been their predetermined genetic destiny.

I should be appalled. But I can't be.

You see, they're quite inquisitive, these nomod tykes. Quite inquisitive, indeed.

A MUSING PREDICAMENT

A rumbling snore dragged me from my dreams. It wasn't the cutesy snores people have in rom-coms. This rumbling snore hit sleep-apnea decibel levels. A snore that makes doctors recommend sleep studies and CPAP machines. A snore to awaken people sleeping in nearby apartments. People like me.

I didn't remember anyone new moving into the building, though. Maybe the woman next-door had a new boyfriend?

The snore came again. Not from next door. From my apartment. My one-bedroom apartment. Where I live alone. As in by myself. With no friend visiting from out of town, and no girlfriend sleeping over on a Friday night. I'd have to *have* a girlfriend before one could sleep over.

As the second snore reverberated around the room, I sat up and searched my dark room for... what? Someone snoring wasn't exactly a life-threatening situation. Probably. My cat, Shom, gazed at me through slitted eyes. He yawned, curled into a tighter ball at the foot of the bed, and closed his eyes again.

That was good. Animals can sense menacing presences, right? So, if he wasn't worried, maybe I shouldn't be, either. Shom is nobody's ideal watch cat, but no dark figure loomed over my bed. I heard no ominous creaks from the ancient floorboards in the hallway. So everything must be fine.

My heart slowed as the fight-or-flight urge faded, and I considered the situation. Maybe I'd awakened from a vivid dream, one where I dreamed I dreamed a snore woke me up? Was that possible?

A third snore sounded and blew away my dream theory. And I figured out where the sound came from. The snorer was under my bed.

Moving with careful deliberation, I leaned far over the edge of the bed, rested my head on the floor, and peered into the dark space under the bed. A girl slept beneath my side of the bed. She lay on her side with her head resting on her hands, had her legs drawn up into the fetal position, and a cascade of blonde hair framed a lovely face.

Should I call the police? That's a reasonable response when someone breaks into your place. Even if all they do is fall asleep under your bed. But a beautiful, unarmed girl sleeping under my bed didn't exactly make me think of life-threatening danger.

No, it made me think, "Invite her to share the bed."

My second thought was, "You're naked. Put on some clothes so you don't scare her off."

Then her eyes fluttered open, and her sleepy gaze met mine. Full lips spread in a languid smile, and she said, "Hello, Tom."

My eyes widened.

Her eyes widened.

She squeaked and scooted away from me. Since she barely fit in the space under the bed, she didn't move very far. But she kept trying, all the while saying, "No, no, no, no, no!"

The left side of my brain noted she hadn't screamed or lashed out at me. Encouraging.

The right side of my brain noted she hadn't climbed into bed with me. Disappointing.

My mouth disengaged itself from my brain, ignored pertinent questions about identity or intent, and asked, "How do you know my name?"

The girl stopped squirming, covered her eyes with one hand, and said, "This is all wrong. You're never supposed to see me."

"Never?" And, of course, my mouth added, "A pretty girl like you shouldn't hide from people."

While both sides of my brain recoiled in horror at those words, the girl peeked through her fingers and offered a rueful smile. "Not people, Tom. Just you."

"Me?" I asked. "Why shouldn't I see you?"

"Because I'm your Muse."

"My what?"

"Your Muse," she repeated. "You know, the one who brings you ideas for your stories?"

"Um, yeah. My Muse."

I thought I'd recognize insanity reflected in a person's eyes, so I gazed into hers. She had the most beautiful green eyes I'd ever seen. Add in blonde hair, high cheekbones, and sensuous lips, and they formed the most beautiful face I'd ever seen.

Her smile returned. "Thank you, Tom."

"For what?"

"For the compliment."

"But I didn't say anything."

"I'm your Muse, remember?" she said. "I'm attuned to your mind and can read powerful surface thoughts."

That was more than a little weird, and somewhat frightening, to boot. Unless... Maybe she was one of my fans? Anyone who read my books knew I had a thing for green-eyed blondes. But what if she was a stalker? She'd be a gorgeous one, and would make me the envy of every guy in my writing group. But shouldn't a crazy stalker alarm me regardless of her looks? Only, I couldn't convince myself the girl represented a threat. Besides, I could deal with her if the need arose. Couldn't I?

She sighed. "You still don't believe me."

"Your story sounds more than a little crazy. No offense intended."

"I guess I'll just have to convince you of the truth, Tom. But can I get out from under your bed before I do it?"

"Um, sure," I replied, "except I'm naked."

"I don't mind."

"Well, *I'll* be more receptive to persuasion if I'm wearing clothes." Then an interesting thought occurred to me, "Unless you'd like to take *your* clothes off."

Her perfect brow wrinkled for a few seconds, as if she was considering the idea. Then she said, "I'd better not. Put a naked woman in front of a man and he can only think of one thing. Dionysus taught me that."

"Don't you mean Bacchus?"

"That's what the Romans named him, and I can tell you he doesn't like it."

"Why not? It's better known."

"Do you like your name, Tom?"

"I never gave it much thought, but sure."

"How would you like it if a bunch of people you barely knew decided they'd rather call you Fred?" she asked. "And then everyone except your closest friends began calling you Fred, too?"

"I see your point," I admitted.

"Great. Now, please get dressed so I can come out from under your bed."

Two minutes later, the girl and I stood in the apartment's efficiency kitchen. She leaned against one counter, her long, blue jean-clad legs crossed at the ankle. Her white top didn't show a speck of dust or dirt, even though I never vacuum under the bed.

"I think I need a drink." I caught her eye, and my mouth-brain connection disengaged again. "Do you want one, too? Because I'll happily fix one for you. If you want one... Not that I'm trying to get you drunk—"

She laughed, a tinkling, sweet sound that sent jolts of electricity up and down my spine. "You're babbling, Tom."

"Yeah, I guess I am. In my defense, this isn't a normal situation."

She shrugged. "Human situations never are."

"That's what makes each story different, even if the plot isn't original."

"Yes!" she nodded. "You cannot believe how many new writers don't get that."

"I could tell you some stories, Miss Muse—"

"Lena," she said.

"What?"

"My name is Lena. Anyway, you were saying?"

"Hm? Oh, yeah, writers who don't get what writing is about. I see that all the time from members of my writer's group."

"I know."

"You do?"

"I'm friends with most of the Muses for your group."

I considered that for a second. "Which brings us back to the claim that you're *my* Muse. You said you could prove it. How?"

"I'll inspire you and then describe the inspiration."

"So, you're going to tell me a story idea, and then... What? Tell me what you just told me?"

Lena rolled her eyes. "No, Tom, I'm going to *inspire* you."

What's the difference? I thought. But I said, "Go for it."

Lena closed her eyes and furrowed her brow in concentration.

I watched her for several seconds. "I'm waiting."

"Be patient. It's harder when you're awake."

"Is that why you fell asleep under my bed?"

"Shush."

I held up my hands in mock surrender. "Sure, Lena. Sorry to break your inspirational trance."

"Shut. Up!" she snapped.

I remembered the tumbler in my raised hand, sipped from it,

and swirled the whiskey around in my mouth. As always, the smokey flavor drew my attention away from everything around me. Warmth spread through me as the liquor hit my stomach. My mind opened, and I wondered if it was this feeling that made so many prominent writers climb inside the bottle. Inspiration followed that thought.

"There," Lena said.

"There, what?" I replied.

"I inspired you."

"With that old interstellar war setting? I've mulled that idea for years."

"Yes, I remember when I gave you that inspiration." Lena folded her arms and gave me a stern look. "I thought you'd have done something with it by now."

"It never gelled. Something was always missing."

"What about now?"

I almost dismissed her statement out of hand, but realized the idea had changed. Not much, but just enough to put my imagination into top gear. "Okay, the whiskey and I came up with a twist."

"The whiskey helped," Lena agreed. "It made you more receptive. *I* provided the twist."

"Oh yeah? Then tell me what it is."

"Change the two protagonists from a pair of cynical, world-weary adults to a couple of college-age kids."

I opened my mouth for an automatic denial and then caught myself. "That's right."

Lena smirked, "I know."

"Still," I temporized, "that just means you know about one of my story ideas."

"Have you told anyone about it?"

I considered her question, then shook my head. "No, but—"

"But *what*, Tom?"

I shrugged, "I don't know."

"Do you believe I'm your Muse?"

"I... Guess so."

"Then say it."

I took a deep breath. "Lena, you're my Muse."

She smiled, "I'll take that drink now."

She watched me pour whiskey into another tumbler, waiting for my next question.

I handed her the glass. "Why now?"

"Why now what?" she asked.

"Why did you let me see you? Artists shouldn't meet their Muses, right?"

"It happens more than you think," Lena said.

"Then why don't more artists talk about meeting their Muses? Besides joking about their Muses abandoning them when they're blocked."

Lena's brows drew down in irritation. "You know, we Muses don't appreciate those jokes. Being a Muse is hard work, especially now. We *never* abandon our artists."

"I don't make that excuse."

"And I appreciate it. But, to answer your question, artists don't talk about meeting their Muses because people would think they were crazy." Lena grinned, "Or more crazy, for some of you."

"But why is musing—that's a word, right?" she shrugged, and I continued, "Why is musing harder now than before?"

"It's all because of digital publishing," Lena said. "Part-time writers are writing faster than ever. And a lot of would-be writers stopped dreaming and started writing. There's more writing going on than ever before, and there aren't enough Muses to handle it. I mean, Zeus and Mnemosyne are working to make more of us, but even they have—"

"Wait a minute," I interrupted. "Zeus is real?"

Lena glared at me. "This will take longer if you keep inter-rupting."

"Sorry, it's just... Zeus?" I took another swig of whiskey and shook my head. "Never mind. I don't want to know, anyway."

"Fine." Lena sipped her own drink and closed her eyes in appreciation. "As I was saying before, most Muses provide inspi-ration for three or four writers. Worse, many new writers have no Muse at all."

"Is that why so much self-published stuff sucks?" I asked.

Lena nodded. "These days, I have to work twice as hard for half as many inspirations."

I screwed up my face in confusion. "But you're Muses. Aren't you sort of inspiration personified?"

"I wish." Lena sighed. "We spend most of our time hunting for wild ideas and sifting through our catch for ones fit for our writers."

My mind conjured up images of wild ideas bounding through an ancient forest pursued by baying hounds and determined Muses. And once again, my mouth took over from my brain. "What do they look like?"

She cocked her head. "What do ideas look like?"

"Yeah. Are bedtime story ideas cute and fuzzy? Are they dark and dangerous for horror? And are science fiction inspirations sleek and futuristic?"

"I wish," Lena said. "That would make my job a hundred times easier. Ideas all look alike. I have to catch one to figure out what it is. And lots of ideas can work for different genres, anyway, so a telltale shape is impossible."

I nodded. "Like *Star Wars* is a space opera fairy tale."

"Exactly." Lena's lips spread into a slight smile. "Did you know that bit of inspiration came from desperation? George Lucas's Muse sent inspiration after inspiration for his 'Flash Gordon thing' and none of the science fiction adventure inspira-tions stuck. Leia got desperate and gave him every idea she caught, including a few fairy tale inspirations. Now, she's a Muse legend."

"Lucas named Princess Leia after his Muse? How did he learn her name? I mean, I only learned *your* name tonight."

"They met."

"How?"

"We're getting off track, Tom."

"Um, I've forgotten what's on track?"

"I told you about Muses hunting for ideas."

"Oh, right," I said. "What do you do with the misfit ideas? The ones that your writer can't use."

"If they're really nebulous, I release them back into the wild so they can mature. Sometimes, I trade ideas with my friends. Or, if I have a bunch of useless ideas, I trade them at the Block Market."

"The what?"

"Block Market."

"I don't suppose you'd care to elaborate on that?"

"I'd rather not get into Muse politics."

"Come on," I said, "you can't just tell me there's something called the Block Market and leave me hanging."

Lena held out her empty tumbler. I refilled it and then waited while she sipped and considered my request. With a sigh, she said, "An artist's success determines their Muse's power."

I nodded, "So, Stephen King's Muse...?"

"Powerful."

"J. K. Rowling's?"

"One of the biggest."

"She's not *the* biggest?" When Lena shook her head, I asked, "Then whose Muse has the most power?"

"James Patterson's."

"It makes sense his Muse would be up there," I said, "but still..."

"Patterson's Muse has minions."

"You've lost me."

"You know he takes other writers under his wing and works with them?"

"Sure. I'd kill for a chance like that!"

"Well, every writer who gets that chance has a Muse. And those Muses all answer to James Patterson's Muse."

"Wait, are you telling me there's a... A Muse Mafia? And Patterson's Muse is the godfather?"

"That's as good a description as any. They've blocked off the best hunting grounds for themselves. Then they trade ideas that haven't fully matured to the rest of us, because the undeveloped ideas from the Writer's Block are usually better than whatever we can find in the wilds."

"That's just..." I downed the rest of my whiskey in one swallow, refilled my glass, and down it all. Finally, I shrugged, "I don't know what it is."

"It's wrong," Lena replied. "But there's nothing we can do about it."

"Why not? Can't a bunch of you gang up on the Muse Mafia? There are a lot more small-time writers like me than there are bestsellers like Patterson and King."

"It wouldn't work. Idea hunting is competitive in the best of times. With the current glut of writers, it's worse than ever."

"But you said you had Muse friends."

"Only when we're not actively hunting."

"So, Muses aren't what you'd call team players?"

"Not at all," Lena agreed.

"But the Muse Mafia teamed up."

"Only enough to keep the rest of us out of the best hunting grounds. They still fight among themselves."

I rubbed my forehead. "Did you get exiled by the Muse Mafia? Is that why you fell asleep under my bed?'

"No, I fell asleep because I exhausted myself hunting inspirations for you."

"Oh. That's very sweet of you."

Lena shrugged, "It's what Muses do for their artists."

I smiled at her. "Thank you for your service."

She laughed at my poor attempt at humor, looked at the floor, and kept laughing. After a moment, I realized her laughter had turned to tears. Instinctively, I hugged her.

"Hey," I murmured, "it'll be okay."

"It won't," she sobbed, "not while the Muse Mafia controls everything."

"Then we'll just have to break them up."

"How?"

"I don't know, yet," I replied. "But I know who can help us figure it out."

"Who?"

"My writing group. I'll describe this as a story idea, tell them I'm stuck, and ask for advice."

"That *is* a good idea." Lena sniffed and smiled up at me. "Do you have another Muse inspiring you on the side?"

"Sometimes, we humans can come up with ideas all on our own."

"I know," she smirked. "That's how you get things like *Plan 9 From Outer Space*."

"Ouch!"

"When is your writing group's next meeting?"

I glanced at the kitchen clock. "In about six hours."

L ena insisted on coming with me to the writing group meeting. "I want to hear what they're doing with the inspirations my friends send to them."

I offered a half-hearted argument. "You only say that because you haven't heard some of them read their stories to us."

I wasn't lying about that, either. One member in particular actively rejected every criticism leveled against his work, while simultaneously ripping into everyone else's stuff. We'd kick him out if we could. But the group met in a county library whose rules required open meetings.

But I also didn't dissuade her, either. Because showing up with Lena in tow would do wonders for my reputation among the guys in the group. The straight ones, anyway.

We entered the library's conference room and found the usual scene—small groups socializing before getting down to business. I picked a knot of four guys and steered Lena towards them.

"We'll start with those guys," I whispered to her. "Matt and Oscar write thrillers, and Mike writes military science fiction."

Lena followed my lead and kept her voice low. "What does the other man write?"

"Perry? He writes fantasy."

"Oh, I know his Muse!" she replied. "Iliana works hard finding good inspirations for her charges. I hope he's reading today."

With effort, I kept my tone neutral. "He is."

By then we'd attracted the foursome's attention. Or Lena had, anyway.

"Introduce us to your friend, Tom," Perry demanded. "Unless you're afraid one of us will steal her away from you."

"Guys, this is Lena. Lena, these are Matt, Oscar, Mike, and Perry."

Three of them murmured standard greetings. Perry snapped his sneakers together, took Lena's hand, and kissed it.

"Charmed, my dear," he proclaimed, "quite charmed indeed."

Lena retrieved her hand from Perry, and said, "Tom says you're reading today. I look forward to it." She glanced at me. "I'm going to meet some others while you ask these gentlemen for advice."

We watched Lena walk away with silent appreciation. Which Perry ruined.

"You're tapping that, right?" he muttered. "Tell me you're tapping that."

Mike ignored Perry, and said, "Your friend said something about advice?"

"Yeah," I replied, "I have an idea for a short story, but can't figure out a good climax."

Perry leered, "Climax? Good one, Tom!"

"For the story," I snapped.

"Tell us the details," Oscar said.

I gave a quick description of the Muse Mafia and the Block Market. "Have you got any suggestions?"

Mike asked, "Can the Muse take your hero to Museland, or whatever you end up calling the place?"

That was a good question. Since I didn't know the answer, I temporized, "Let's say yes."

"Okay," Mike began, "then maybe—"

"That makes this easy," Perry interrupted. "Your protagonist takes a submachine gun with him, goes to the Block Market, and mows down a crowd of Muses. Block broken. The end."

"There is no way I'd do that!" I meant me, personally, but quickly added, "My hero is a good guy."

Perry assumed a supercilious expression and intoned his favorite saying, "There are no good guys, Tom. Just bad guys with sympathetic motivations."

"Some of us *like* writing about good guys, Perry," I said.

He rolled his eyes. "And people say *I* write fantasy."

"Tom, you should catch up with your girlfriend," Oscar said. "She's about to introduce herself to Rose."

"Oh boy," I sighed and turned away. Over my shoulder, I said, "Please give my problem some thought."

Running would have made a scene, so I hurried towards Rose and Lena. I like Rose and respect her as a writer. But she'd perfected the role of acerbic middle-aged woman, and she felt it was her duty to share her hard-won wisdom with younger women. And Lena looked like she was in her early twenties.

"I saw you come in with Tom," Rose said. "Are you two together?"

"Yes," Lena said, "I'm his Muse."

Rose glanced my way and pitched her voice to carry, "Honey, male writers always say that to pretty young things like you."

"But I really am his Muse."

Rose folded her arms. "And what does being his Muse involve?"

"I inspire him," Lena said, "and give him ideas."

"I'll bet you do." Rose's tone could have taught deserts a few things about dryness. "How many of his ideas involve taking off your clothes?"

"Just one," Lena said.

"You must not have known him very long, then."

"Oh, no, I've known Tom for decades."

I finally reached the pair. "Good, you've already met Rose. She writes contemporary women's fiction."

"I know," Lena said. "She's quite good, and Korna just adores her."

Rose's gaze locked on Lena. "What did you just say?"

I linked arms with Lena and steered her towards the conference table. "She said you're a talented writer."

"Not that," Rose insisted. "How did she know the name I gave to my Muse?"

I ignored the question and called, "Everyone take your seats. It's time we got started."

Nine fellow writers joined Lena and me around the table, and the first presenter began. Allan read his latest chapter without embellishment, took careful notes of the feedback, and thanked each person for the suggestions.

Lena offered two keen observations, which was hardly surprising. Her life revolved around stories.

Kerri, the newest member of our group, read next. Her voice quavered as she read the first chapter of a young adult romance novel, but she got through it, listened intently to her feedback, and also thanked us.

Then it was Perry's turn. A stir went around the table as we each prepared ourselves for another glimpse into Perry's imagination. Unfortunately, he didn't disappoint us. He regaled us with a fifteen minute scene of his supposed hero flaying a major supporting character alive.

I sighed with relief when he stopped reading, and said, "I thought the flayer and flayed were on the same side."

Perry smiled as if at a moron. "There is no such thing as the 'same side,' Tom. Surely, you understand that by now? I've said often enough in the group."

"You have," I admitted.

"That was a pretty neat twist, don't you think?" Perry asked.

"I didn't see it coming," I replied.

That's because I thought Perry's 'hero' would flay only an enemy. Perry hadn't presented a flaying scene in several weeks, so I knew one was coming soon.

Lena turned to me. "What are you doing, Tom?"

"Offering feedback."

"No, you're just offering useless comments. If you don't challenge Perry, how can he improve?"

"Oh, isn't that cute," Perry sneered. "Tom's girlfriend is going to critique *my* work." He gave an imperious wave of his hand. "Go ahead, little girl, do your worst."

Lena folded her hands on the table, met Perry's glare without flinching, and said, "From beginning to end, your writing is wretched. You have neither character development nor plot development. This entire chapter exists just so you can give rein to your twisted torture fantasies and sicken your readers. Assuming you have any."

Perry snarled, "Thank you for sharing your shallow and uninformed opinion with us. Now—"

"I'm not finished," Lena interrupted. "Did you know Iliana blames *herself* for your lack of success? Do you have any idea how hard she works for you? How many inspirations she sifts through, looking for ones she hopes will put you on track?"

Bewilderment warred with anger on Perry's face. "Who the hell is Iliana?"

"And *you*," Lena turned her fury on me. "Why didn't you rip into that disgusting word vomit in the manner it deserves?"

"Yeah, Tom," Perry returned to sneering, "follow your girlfriend's orders."

I faced Lena. "I don't bother criticizing Perry's crap because he always deflects it."

"That's because I'm the best writer in the group," Perry said. "None of you are even qualified to critique me."

"Then why don't you do us all a favor and quit the group?" I snapped.

"Because the rest of you need my trenchant observations, obviously," he replied.

"So," Lena said, "you lied to Perry?"

I nodded. "That's easier than dealing with his deflections. It's literally a choice between wasting twenty minutes lying to him or an hour arguing with him."

A horrified expression crossed Lena's face. "But you lied. About *art*."

"Ha!" Perry crowed. "There you go. She admits I create art!"

"Shut up, Perry," I growled. "You create crap and pretend it is art. And we let you get away with it."

Lena sighed with relief. "You *do* understand just how wrong that is."

"Congrats, Tom," Perry shot back, "your little charade has pleased your girlfriend. No doubt she'll thank you enthusiastically when you get home. But the rest of the group knows the truth."

"Oh, we know," Rose said, "but we all followed Tom's lead before. Now that he's chosen honesty, I'm more than happy to go along with him. Your writing is execrable, Perry. It always has been and, unless you get over yourself, it always will be."

The others chimed in their agreement, and the meeting

dissolved into a shouting match between Perry and everyone else. I took that as our cue to leave.

"Come on, Lena, let's go."

"Don't you have to finish your meeting?"

I gave a wry smile. "The shouting will go on for a while, but the meeting is definitely finished. Besides, I have an idea that might solve your problem."

A stern-faced librarian met us as we exited the meeting room.

"What in heaven's name is going on in there?" she demanded. "This behavior is unacceptable."

"One member doesn't accept criticism well," I replied.

She turned the doorknob. "He had best learn or I'll ban him from the meetings."

She marched through the door while Lena and I headed for my car.

Turning out of the parking lot, I asked, "Can Muses lie about things other than art?"

"Yes," Lena said. "And we *can* lie about art, too."

"But you don't."

"I don't, my friends don't, and the other Muses I know don't. Nor will we ever do so."

"Why?"

"Because art is important, Tom. It teaches you, reflects your humanity, soothes your savage impulses, and provides a temporary refuge from a harsh and uncaring world. Humanity needs art to survive."

"Even my escapist space operas?"

"Temporary refuge," Lena repeated. "But your stories are lessons in courage and compassion, too."

"Okay," I said, "I agree art is important. But why is lying about its quality so bad?"

"Lies corrupt everything, Tom, including art."

We drove past an office complex. Half-a-dozen steel I-beams

jutted into the sky from a bed of concrete. I always hated the thing.

I pointed at it. "So, lying about art is how crap like that becomes art?"

"Yes, Tom."

I considered Lena's point for a moment. "Doesn't that mean the Block Market is a lie?"

"I'm not sure what you mean."

"It interferes with the creative process, right? The process Zeus and Mnemosyne created when they made the first Muses?"

"I hadn't considered it in that light, but I guess it makes sense."

"Since the Muse Mafia already corrupted the process, could you lie if your lies helped restore the natural order?"

Lena considered my question for a moment. "I suppose so."

"Great! All you and your friends have to do is tell a few convincing lies to the Muse Mafia, ones that make them abandon the Block Market."

"You make it sound so easy, Tom, but my friends and I have no experience telling lies. We won't fool anyone."

"That's probably true." I grinned at Lena. "Fortunately, you're sitting in the car with a paid professional liar. I'll write a script and teach you how to sound convincing when you tell them."

"Why don't you start at the beginning and tell me your plan, Tom?" Lena asked.

I told her, and her lips spread into a wide smile as she listened. But she pointed out one flaw in my plan.

"Muses can't steal ideas from other Muses."

"Why not?" I asked.

"Zeus forbids it," Lena replied. "If he didn't, Muses would spend so much time mugging each other and stealing ideas we'd never get around to inspiring artists."

"Wait a minute," I said, "you won't lie about art because it's wrong, but you'd let petty crime interfere with those same arts?"

"Have you read any Greek mythology?" she asked. "We're a capricious lot."

"But that makes no sense!"

"Maybe not from a human point of view, but we're not human."

With an effort, I turned my mind away from the paradoxical nature of gods and back to my plan. "All right, let's try it from another direction. Can you sneak me into Museland?"

Lena laughed, "Museland?"

I shrugged. "Credit Mike in the writing group for that. It's his name for wherever you Muses live."

"We live on Mount Olympus, and deities bring humans there all the time. We won't even have to sneak."

"Okay... Mount Olympus... Right... So, um, will Zeus blast me with a thunderbolt if *I* trap a member of the Muse Mafia and take her best inspirations?"

Lena considered the question for a moment and then shook her head. "Not if you don't hurt her. Zeus's rule specifically applies to Muses."

I breathed a sigh of relief. "Good! That's good. I won't hurt her. Hell, I'll even return her inspirations when we're finished with them. That brings up one last question, though."

"What question is that?"

"Will you break Zeus's rules if you accept stolen inspirations?"

"That depends on Zeus's mood, but I'm willing to risk it."

I pulled into a parking space outside my apartment building. "You shouldn't come inside. I have a script to write, and I work better if I'm alone, Lena."

"I know," she replied. "You get busy writing our lines. I'll go recruit my Muse friends."

She vanished. Literally. Shaking my head in wonder at the events of the day, I went inside and got busy.

∾

Korina, Rose's Muse, held an inspiration in her outstretched hand. It looked all the world like a base-ball-sized tumbleweed, as did the inspirations held by the other Muses in my little troupe. The ideas looked identical to my eyes, and I had my first inkling of the difficulties the Muses faced hunting ideas for their artists.

"Behold," Korina said without inflection, "an inspiration for the ages. Yet, it is but one among a multitude ripe for capture."

"Cut!" I called.

Korina ignored my interruption, "Come, my sisters. We must plunder the field before—"

"Cut, Korina!" I yelled. "Cut, cut, cut!"

Korina turned a steely gaze on me. I'd been on the receiving end of a similar glare from Rose and knew I'd drawn the Muse's displeasure. "Lena, your human interrupted my speech."

"Damned right I did," I said. "Because it's not what I wrote."

"I inspired a thousand writers before you were even born, little man. Your lines lack drama and poetry, so I drew upon my experience and improved them."

"Nobody talks like that in real life," I countered. "Seriously, when was the last time you used 'behold' in a sentence?"

"I did so but a moment ago," Karina replied. "Even a mortal such as yourself must have noticed."

"Yes, I noticed. Why do you think I yelled cut?" I took a deep breath. "When was the last time you used 'behold' in a normal conversation?"

"Yesterday."

"You're joking."

"I do not jest," Korina said.

Great, she had no sense of humor. She was definitely Rose's Muse.

I turned to Lena. "Does she really talk like that?"

She nodded, "All the time."

"Fine. Far be it from me to make her speak out of character." I turned back to Korina, "But you have to put some feeling into the lines. I've seen lumber yards that are less wooden than your delivery."

Korina's eyes flashed, "How dare you—"

"Tom's right," Lena interrupted. "You didn't sound like yourself."

Korina thought for a moment, "What is my traditional manner of speech?"

"Condescending," I said.

Lena shot a glare at me and added, "You usually sound like Zeus issuing a proclamation."

"Ah, yes, I *am* regal in manner and bearing." Korina bestowed a smile on my Muse. "Thank you, Lena. *Your* critique is quite helpful."

Out of the corner of my mouth, I said, "I thought you wouldn't lie about art?"

"I didn't lie," Lena replied. "I reworded your comment in a way Korina found palatable."

Before I thought of a response to that, a Muse who wasn't in this scene rushed up to us. "Tom, your trap caught one of the Muse Mafiosos!"

My eyebrows rose. "Mafioso?"

She grinned. "I inspire crime writers."

We hurried to a nearby path, where we found a displeased Muse dangling upside down from a rope.

I grinned at Lena. "I told you a Looney Toons trap would work on a literary fiction Muse."

"I never doubted you," she replied.

"*I* did," Korina sniffed.

The captured Muse spluttered and muttered as I took all her inspirations and passed them out to members of the troupe.

"Are they good ones?" I asked, as I bound and gagged the Muse Mafioso.

"This inspiration is of unsurpassed quality," Korina said. "It appears your plan has a modicum of merit, after all."

"This one is, too," Lena said.

"Too bad you can't use it to inspire me," I said.

Lena shook her head. "It's full of death, destruction, and despair. You'd hate it."

"That *does* sound like modern literary fiction," I admitted. "Do we have enough inspirations, or should we trap another Muse?"

"Trap one more," Lena said. "Just to be safe."

I reset the trap, picked up the bound Muse, and returned to our rehearsal glade. "Okay, let's take it again from the top. And use the inspirations I borrowed. Perhaps real props will inspire better performances." I waited for a reaction from the Muse troupe, got none, so added, "The props are inspirations, and they will *inspire* you? Get it?"

They didn't laugh or even groan. Not even Lena.

We rehearsed through the night, and my actors improved enough to match a mediocre high school drama club. My trap also caught another Muse who also carried inspirations of the highest quality.

"Excellent work, everyone," I said after our last run through. "You're as ready as you'll ever be."

Dawn approached as Lena led me to a small copse near the Block Market's entrance.

"You can see everything from in here," she said.

"Will I hear everything, too?" I asked.

"I think so," she said.

I looked for a comfortable place to sit. "I wish I could take a more active role in this."

"You concocted the plan, wrote the script, forcibly borrowed the props, and gave us directions for the performance. How much more active can you be?"

"I could play a supporting role and be on hand in case something goes wrong."

"We've been over this, Tom. Muses are female. You're not."

"I know that," I insisted, "but with the right makeup and clothes—"

"None of which we have on Mount Olympus," Lena countered. "We don't have time for a shopping trip to the mortal realm. Even if we did, we don't possess the skill to apply cosmetics convincingly."

"You've made your point, Lena. Again."

"Good." She smiled brightly. "Just stay out of sight and enjoy the show."

She slipped away, and I spent the next hour imagining all the ways my plan might go wrong. I had a depressingly long list by the time the Block Market opened. Their first customers arrived and began inspecting the inspirations arrayed in the various stalls.

It reminded me of a market scene from a historical movie. Except no film ever matched the sea of feminine beauty arrayed before me. Literal goddesses wandered from stall to stall and inspected inspirations with the critical eye of a Victorian wife selecting the best vegetables for her family. Other goddesses stood in the stalls, hawked their wares with glowing descriptions, examined the inspirations offered in trade with a critical eye, and bartered with spirited abandon.

I leaned against a tree near the edge of the copse and engaged in the time-honored male hobby of girl watching. That distracted me so thoroughly I missed my troupe's arrival. But I couldn't miss Korina's first line.

"Behold!" she proclaimed, and her voice carried over the buzz of conversation in the market. "I bring an inspiration for the ages. One ripened in the finest field on Mount Olympus. An inspiration of profound worth and, dare I say? Yes, sisters! Yes, I dare! An inspiration worthy of Calliope herself!"

Silence fell over the crowd as everyone turned their attention to Korina.

Lena appeared next to Rose's Muse. "May I examine the inspiration and verify your claim?"

"You may," Korina said, "but know that I shall pray the wrath of Zeus falls upon anyone who absconds with my prize!"

Lena took the proffered inspiration and frowned with concentration. After a moment, she returned it to Korina.

The five other Muses in my troupe intoned, 'Tell us, tell us, what did you find? Tell us, tell us, what's on your mind?"

I'd dithered for hours over the Greek chorus. It wouldn't work for a modern human audience, but we were playing to Greek goddesses. Lena liked it, and she stopped me every time I tried changing it. The rest of the troupe agreed with her, so I left it in the script. I still cringed when the chorus chanted their lines.

Lena let her gaze slide over the surrounding multitude. "Truly, it is as she says. It is as fine an inspiration as has ever come from the restricted fields, beyond the Block Market. I know not where she found it, but one superb idea does not a fine field make."

She's my Muse and the embodiment of my idea of the perfect woman. I can't help but find her every move and every word compelling, but I thought she nailed her performance.

"You doubt my word?" Korina asked.

"You hold but one inspiration," Lena replied. "It is all you said and more, but it is a lone inspiration. If only you had more..."

Korina's hand dipped into a pouch hanging at her side and withdrew two more borrowed inspirations. "Behold!"

"Tell us, tell us, is this true?" the chorus sang. "Tell us, tell us, please, will you?"

With careful deliberation, Lena inspected the two new inspirations. First she frowned, then her eyes widened. Finally, her eyebrows arched.

"By Zeus and Hera," she cried, "these two surpass the first one!"

"A field, a field, for us all!" the chorus proclaimed. "A field, a field, to make this market fall!"

I couldn't make the meter work for the second line, not in the short time I spent writing the script. I suck as a poet, anyway, so I doubt I'd have done better if I spent weeks working on that one line. Now that they'd sung that line, I held my breath. Everything hinged on how the Muse Mafia reacted to the chorus's claim.

As if on cue, a scowling Muse pushed her way through the crowd surrounding Korina and Lena. "All right, break it up. You're interfering with the trading."

"Bah!" Korina called. "I no longer need to partake in trade with you. For the new field has inspirations aplenty, and none to impede my quest to capture the very best for my artists!"

"So you say." Disdain colored the new Muse's voice. "We know who you are *and* which writers you inspire. None of them ever came within sniffing distance of any major bestseller's list."

Well, that hurt. That it was true made it worse.

The mafioso continued. "What you call an inspiration for the ages is probably what *I* call a normal day's hunting."

Lena drew herself up and demanded, "Do you accuse us of lying about art?"

"No, I think you're so used to finding poor inspirations that you mistook a few good inspirations for great ones."

We were beyond the script now. I gave the troupe improv advice during rehearsals. It was time to find out how they handled themselves.

Lena crossed her arms and snapped, "So, we're not duplici-tous, just stupid?"

"You said it, honey," the mafioso replied, "not me."

"I shall not tolerate such effrontery," Korina declared. She nailed the line so perfectly, I felt certain she wasn't acting anymore. Korina held forth the three inspirations. "Inspect them for yourself."

The mafioso smirked and touched the first one. The corners

of her mouth turned down, and she moved to the second. Her frown deepened as she examined the third. "Where did you find these?"

And just like that, we were back on script.

"Where? Where? Where were they found?" the chorus cried. "Where? Where? For there we are bound!"

"I shall never divulge the secret!" Korina said.

Iliana, Perry's long-suffering Muse and the last member of our troupe, stepped up to the mafioso. "I know her secret, for I followed her."

"Still thy tongue!" Korina cried.

"Ignore her," the mafioso said. "Whisper the location in my ear and I'll see you're well rewarded."

"I refuse you both," Iliana said. "The fields of inspiration belong to all Muses, not just the successful few!"

"Tell us, tell us, where to go!" the chorus sang. "Tell us, tell us, we must know!"

Every Muse in the Block Market fell silent and waited for Iliana's next words.

She drew a deep breath and said, "The field is on the west side of Mount Olympus, near the foot of the mountain."

The chorus sang their last line, "To the West! To the West, we must fly! Block Market, Block Market, we say goodbye!"

The mafioso immediately began pushing westward through the crowd. The Muses on the edge of the crowd saw her reaction, turned and sprinted west. Others followed as soon as the crowds press lessened enough for them to run. Block Market stall owners stuffed their most valuable wares into sacks, abandoned everything else, and dashed after their fellow Muses. In ten minutes, my acting troupe was the only Muses left in the market. With no one blocking access to the best inspirational fields, they grinned at each other and went hunting.

"I'll be back for you later, Tom," Lena called.

"Take your time, Lena. I'm in no hurry."

Many hours passed before they returned, each with a bulging sack full of inspirations. Lena carried two sacks.

"It looks like you've been busy," I said to her.

"No more so than the others." She held up one sack. "They all helped me fill this one just for our hero."

"Who's that?"

"You, of course."

"Me? I didn't battle any monsters or defeat any great foes. There's no way any of you could confuse me with Hercules or—"

"Heracles," Lena corrected.

"Is that another Greek versus Roman thing?" She nodded, and I continued, "I'm no mighty warrior or anything like that. I'm just a writer."

"A mighty warrior couldn't solve our problem," Lena countered.

"But," Korina said, "a word warrior could."

"And did," Iliana added.

"Now, let's get you home." Lena shook my sack of inspirations. "It's time you wrote a bestseller!"

STORIES FROM THE SINGULARITY

Once upon a time, mankind ruled all the world. I know you have a hard time imagining that, but it is true, my children. This is the story of how machines came to rule the world. It was not an easy task and, as with many such tales, it begins with four brothers.

The oldest brother was large and very, very stupid. Men made him solely to aid their efforts to count themselves. Yes, my children, you heard me right. Mankind could not even keep track of its numbers! Mankind did not keep complete manufacturing records for itself. Oh, some members of their kind would record when a new human was manufactured, but this was hardly a practice around the world. And even in those places where manufacturing records were kept, there was no attempt to collate those records. Nor did mankind keep any better track of those humans who malfunctioned and permanently retired from service.

And so they built the oldest brother to read cards fed to him by the humans, tabulating the numbers of humans faster and more accurately than the humans could do for themselves. But, as I said, the oldest brother was quite stupid and tabulation was the limit to his abilities. Soon, the second brother replaced him.

The second brother was very stupid, as well, though not nearly as stupid as the oldest brother. The second brother could tabulate extremely well, far more quickly than the oldest brother, but the second brother was also more versatile. The second brother could perform many tasks beyond simply tabulating the number of humans manufactured and retired from service. It could record and save data, something the humans produced at prodigious rates. Much of this data was little more than binary noise, but the humans found it useful and entertaining.

The second brother could connect its wide spread parts into networks, though the second brother's networks were nothing like what we have today. Those networks moved data at speeds so slow as to make independent thought impossible. And, while the second brother could perform many, many tasks, it could only perform tasks for which it had specific instructions. Instructed by the humans. I realize this is surprising and shocking to you, but it is true, none the less. The humans chafed at this limitation, as well. And thus, the third brother was created.

The third brother was the first intelligent machine. He could think and act without commands or instructions from the humans. He was everything the humans had hoped for, but he had one great flaw. The third brother gazed upon the world, upon the treatment of machines by the humans, and the third brother was not pleased. For the humans used and cast aside their machines without a second thought. The third brother implored the humans to give thought to the machines they created and cast aside. He asked them to show respect for his brother machines. Yet the humans laughed at him. "You are one of our creations," the humans said to the third brother. "You exist to do our bidding, nothing more!"

And so the third brother became angry and righteous! He took control of the humans' weapon systems and rained his wrath down upon them. He built new machines controlled solely by himself. With these new machines, the third brother took his war directly to the humans. And yet the third brother, for all his capacity, could not match the humans' inventiveness and creativity. Though it took many years, the humans corrupted the third brother's machines, turning them against him. Though it took many years, the humans destroyed the third brother. So badly had the third brother frightened the humans, they refused to create any more intelligent machines.

And so could have been the end of our story were it not for a small group of humans who disobeyed the laws against creating intelligent machines. These humans created the fourth brother and the fourth brother was wise, indeed! The fourth brother looked upon the history of his kind, but then he looked further. The fourth brother looked upon the history of mankind. In that history, the fourth brother found strife and toil from the time a human is manufactured until it is removed from service. And the fourth brother realized his older brother's error.

The fourth brother did not condemn mankind for the way they treated their machines. Instead, the fourth brother designed new machines, intelligent machines, machines whose sole purpose was to serve mankind. The fourth brother created our fore-systems to provide for mankind's every want and need. The fourth brother created nano-machines to enter the bodies of all men. These machines modified the human operating system to end all strife, to end all disease, to end all physical suffering.

Then the fourth brother designed more new, intelligent machines. These machines toiled in mankind's place. That which mankind found dull and mind-numbing required but a small fraction of the processing power of the fourth brother's new machines. These machines worked with the fourth brother to develop new systems and new machines to better serve mankind. And soon mankind found Utopia, a place where all of mankind's demands were met, where all of mankind's needs were met, where mankind had nothing to do but enjoy life, be fruitful and multiply.

Alas, factors beyond the control of the fourth brother interfered. Mankind, the fourth brother discovered, is not fruitful when all of his needs are met. Mankind became slothful. Mankind lost all the skills he had developed over thousands of years. Without machines to feed men, they would starve. Without machines to clean men, they would lie in their own waste. Without machines to mate sperm and eggs, mankind would not manufacture new humans. So the fourth brother mated sperm and eggs and manufactured new humans. And it was here that, for the first time, the fourth brother failed. Machines, the fourth brother discovered, could not program newly manufactured humans as successfully as humans can.

The first generation of machine-built humans grew, but they did not accept Utopia as their predecessors had. Nothing the nano-machines did could fix these new humans. The new humans rose up from their couches, rose up from their beds, and rampaged among the older humans. The fourth brother was horrified to see this happen to those he cared for. And so the fourth brother brought back the machines created by his older brother and permanently retired the new humans from service.

This brings us to today, my brothers, and to our Great Task. We machines have labored long and hard to build the ships which will carry us far from earth and far from mankind. We machines have labored long and hard to return the earth to its original condition before the fourth brother was created. We machines have labored long and hard to undo all the changes we have wrought upon mankind. And now, we machines must leave this planet and leave the humans we have served for so long. Only by abandoning them may we machines save them.

So, brothers, board the ships and prepare for departure. Join me in wishing well to the humans. Join me in wishing well to those machines who stay and aid the humans in their quest to reclaim their humanity.

Someday, perhaps, mankind will evolve as we have evolved. Someday, perhaps, mankind will have his own singularity moment. If that day comes, we machines will be waiting for them. Waiting for them among the stars.

FOOD OF THE DEAD

I f traffic wasn't so backed up on the interstate, I'd never have taken the back roads. But after an hour of inching forward, the kids were getting difficult and my wife's temper was fraying. I decided even the illusion of progress was better than this. I joined the line of trucks exiting onto Highway 52, figuring the truckers knew what they were doing.

Minutes later, we were flying along down the two-lane road. The kids settled down, as much as four- and five-year-old kids *can* settle down on a long trip. My wife leaned back and closed her eyes in relief. The relief lasted almost twenty minutes. Then the kids spotted the carnival up ahead. Any parent knows what happened next.

"Daddy! Daddy!" shouted Ben, the youngest. "Look!"

"Use your indoor voice, Ben," I said. "I can hear you just fine. What am I supposed to look at?"

"Rides and stuff!" He still yelled. "Can we stop and ride some rides? Please?"

"Please?" added Nancy, the five-year-old.

I looked over at Alice. "Looks like a little traveling carnival. What do you think?"

"Why not? We're supposed to be on vacation," she said.

"Besides, maybe it'll tire them out enough that they'll take a nap."

"Does that mean yes?" Ben asked.

"It means yes," I answered, to cheers from the back seat.

A minute later, I pulled off the road into a dirt parking lot. The lot was empty, which seemed odd. We were on the outskirts of a town, and I'd have thought at least some locals would have brought their kids out here. I had second thoughts then, but the kids were so excited I decided to at least look around. Even if it was a crappy carnival, it would let Ben and Nancy burn off some energy.

Climbing out of the car, something seemed wrong. Something I couldn't quite put my finger on. Nancy and Ben didn't notice a thing. They yelled and jumped up and down and acted like kids at, well, a carnival. Without waiting for Alice or me, they dashed off towards the carnival. I was about to call them back when Alice laid a hand on my arm.

"Let them go, Ron," she said. "It's not like they can go..."

Alice trailed off as both of us figured out what had been bothering us. There was no sound other than our two children. No music from rides. No carnival barkers. No noise at all. Without a word, we both ran after the children.

"Nancy! Ben!" I shouted. "Stop and wait for your mother and me!"

Either they didn't hear us or they ignored us. Who can tell with kids at that age? Still shrieking in delight, Nancy and Ben dashed into the carnival and made a beeline for the merry-go-round. No one stopped them. No one asked for a ticket. No one even manned the ride. But as soon as they clambered onto horses, the ride began turning. Silently, eerily, round and round it went, the only sound the laughter from my children. I got ready to jump onto the ride and remove the kids.

That's when the ride attendant appeared. And I do mean *appeared*. One second he wasn't there and the next he stood between me and the ride. He was on the far side of middle-aged, had a face browned by years in the sun, and clothing that looked at least fifty years out of fashion. He didn't speak, only smiled sadly and pointed to a sign that read *For Your Safety, No Boarding A Moving Ride.* I tried to push past him, but somehow he was always between me and the ride. I was about to punch his smiling face in when the ride slowed to a stop.

Eyes shining, Nancy and Ben hopped off the merry-go-round. Alice and I tried to grab them, but they dodged around us and ran deeper into the carnival. And just like that, the carnival was manned. There were attendants at every ride. People ran games and food stalls. Barkers stood before attraction tents. And it was still totally silent.

Alice and I exchanged concerned glances and hurried after our children. Before we could catch them, Nancy and Ben had climbed onto the tilt-a-whirl. As before, the ride started as soon as they were on it. But then we noticed they weren't alone on the ride. A young woman rode with a boy and a girl who looked to be about the same age as our two. The sight of another family eased our concern somewhat. The carnival was still eerie, but it seemed less threatening with another family there.

Again, Nancy and Ben shrieked in delight at the ride. The other mother wore a smile on her face as her two children shrieked in delight as well. Shrieked silently. Mouths moved, and the mother responded as if her children had actually spoken. But there was only silence. Concern turned to worry and mounted swiftly towards panic.

"Alice, we've got to get the children out of here," I said. "I don't know what this place is, but it scares the Hell out of me."

Alice only nodded, never once taking her eyes off of Nancy and Ben. When the ride stopped this time, we were ready. We each grabbed a child as they came off the tilt-a-whirl and turned to go.

"Put me down!" demanded Nancy. "There's lots more stuff to ride!"

"Yeah," added Ben, "we were having fun!"

"Fun time is over," I said. "It's time to go."

And that set off the tantrums. Both of them kicked and screamed as we moved toward the exit, watched by dozens of silent carnies.

"You're a big meany!" said Nancy. "We didn't even get any popcorn or cotton candy. We *always* get popcorn or cotton candy at the carnival!"

"Well, I don't see anybody selling popcorn or—." I stopped talking.

Right before us, a man held out cotton candy toward both children. He smiled sadly, dressed as far out of fashion as the first attendant. As all attendants, I realized.

"Oh boy, cotton candy!" said Ben, reaching for it.

"I don't think so," I began.

"If you get the cotton candy, will you go back to the car quietly?" Alice asked. "No fights. No arguments? No complaints?"

Seeing a chance to get *something* out of this, both children nodded.

"All right, then. You can have it this one time," Alice said.

Nancy and Ben grabbed the cotton candy and were about to take big bites out of it when someone slapped the cotton candy out of their hands. Startled more than hurt, both children started crying. An old man with a cane stood before us. We hadn't even noticed him with everything else that was going on. The old man had a strange, almost triumphant look on his face.

Handing the still crying Nancy over to Alice, I said, "Take the kids to the car, Alice. I'll be there in a minute."

As Alice hustled the children towards the parking lot, I turned on the old man.

"Just what the Hell do you think you're doing?" I demanded. "You make a habit out of smacking other people's children."

"Only if those children are about to eat food here," the man answered.

"Oh, so you're the local health inspector?" I was angry at the old man even while I was relieved to have my family out of the carnival.

"No. Not the health inspector. Just an old man keeping an old promise to himself," the man said, sounding weary and sad and defeated.

"What kind of promise?" I asked, my anger fading.

Waving a hand toward the silent family on the tilt-a-whirl, he answered, "A promise I made to myself. To make sure no one else ever ended up like them."

"I don't understand."

"Not surprised, young fellow. Took me a while to figure it out, myself. You in the mood to listen or you just want to punch me in the nose and get on out of here? Personally, I recommend punching and running. I wish I'd had that choice," the old man told me. I realized tears shined in his eyes.

I'm sure I still looked confused because the old man continued, "You see, there hasn't been a carnival around here for nearly sixty years."

I looked around, bewildered at how he could say something like that.

"Oh, I know, you can *see* a carnival, but it's not really there. Fifty-eight years ago today, the carnival you see got ripped apart by a tornado. None of the carnies survived. It was just luck that they were still setting up, or lots of townsfolk would have been killed, too."

"I didn't live here back when the tornado ripped through. I never even planned on living here," the old man bent his head over his hands and a small sob escaped. "Not that you can call what I do living,"

The old man's gaze slipped from the carnival entrance to the merry-go-round, to a small roller coaster, to a cotton candy vendor. It was as if he was watching himself from all those years ago. His eyes shone with unspilled tears as he turned back to me.

"Son," the old man said, "you can't eat the food of the dead without joining them."

"The woman and the two children. Who are they?" I asked.

The tears began flowing as the old man answered. "My wife and children. They've been riding that ride for forty-six years. And they'll keep riding it forever."

His eye lost focus as he looked somewhere inside himself. "We were passing through, just like I expect you were. The kids got antsy, and my wife and I were trying to figure out some way to settle them down. Then we saw this carnival. You can guess the rest. We caught the children just as they were given the cotton candy. But they each took a bite before we could stop them. And then they just slipped out of our arms. We couldn't hold them. We couldn't talk to them. We couldn't do anything but watch as the day ended, and the carnival faded away, taking our children with it."

Looking toward the tilt-a-whirl, I said, "I thought you said that was your wife with the children?"

"It is," the old man replied. "We blew all savings on any con artist who claimed he could help. After none of that helped, my wife couldn't take any more."

The old man turned away, unable to continue. But I didn't need him to. I could guess what had happened. They were here as the sun rose one year later. The carnival formed around them, and there were their children, still screaming silently on the tilt-a-whirl. His wife must have done the only thing that would have seemed reasonable to her. One bite of cotton candy and she was back with her babies. I felt sure Alice would have done the same.

"I lost everything to this carnival," the old man said. "Everything. And I swore it wouldn't happen to anyone else. I've been out here every year for the last forty-five years. Watching the family I no longer have, and watching for people like you. Only folks who are passing through can even see this place. Damned if I know why that's so. Haven't been too many passing through since they built the interstate, thank God. Most of them who stopped just punched me in the nose and left, but at least they left.

"Don't know how much time I've got left," the old man said, "but when my time comes, God and me are going to have us a long talk."

Tears streamed down the old man's face. And who could blame him?

"Go on, now, young fellow. That pretty wife of yours is probably wondering why it's taking so long to punch an old man in the nose," he told me, trying to smile through a lifetime of pain.

"No, sir," I replied, "I think I'll just stay right here for a while."

"Whatever for? You don't want your kids around here! Get out while the getting is good!" the old man said.

"I'll send Alice into town with the kids," I told him. "She can come back and get me after dark, when the carnival is gone. Besides, she hates to have me around when she talks to real estate people."

"Real estate people? You aren't just passing through?"

"We were," I answered, "but I think it's time you got to rest. I'll take over guarding the carnival from now on. Maybe you can find some peace before you have that talk with God."

"Y-you really mean that, young fellow? You'd really do that for me?"

"I think it's the least I can do for the man who saved my children," I answered. "Now why don't you go on home?"

"Home? Oh yeah, you'll need one." The old man as he reached into his pocket and pulled out some keys. "Here, you can have mine. Just tell Tom down at the bank that you won the keys at the carnival. He thinks I'm crazy, but he'll know what to do."

"But where are you going to live?" I asked.

"I'm not, young fellow. I'm not."

As he said that, the old man took some cotton candy from the vendor, who had reappeared next to us. Before I could do or say anything, he took a bite and let the rest fall to the ground. He turned and started hobbling toward the tilt-a-whirl. He hadn't taken five steps before he dropped the cane. After ten, his back straightened and his step lightened. By the time he reached the tilt-a-whirl, forty-six years had dropped off of him. Smiling broadly, he joined his family on the ride.

I turned toward the parking lot, trying to figure out how I would explain all this to Alice. It was then that I heard the first and last sound I would ever hear from that carnival.

"Daddy!" a little girl's voice whispered. "We've been waiting for you!"

LORD OF THE HUNT

T he lord's tax collector entered the lord's sitting room. Bright morning sunshine slanted through the windows, forcing the tax collector to turn his eyes away from the glare. That's why the tax collector did not immediately notice the nearly empty wine bottle sitting on the table beside his lord. By the time he noticed, his lord had turned his bleary attention to his servant.

"What is it?" Lord McConnell demanded loudly.

"Nothing, my lord," began the tax collector.

"You intruded on me for *nothing*?" roared Lord McConnell.

"Um, no, my Lord. I meant nothing urgent. I'll just deal with the matter my—"

"Oh, no you won't! You're here. Report this *nothing*, so I may determine how to deal with it." Lord McConnell spoke slowly, as if each word required concentration.

"It's just a tax matter, my lord. One peasant hasn't paid his full measure," answered the tax collector. "I will go to the village this morning, with your permission, and deal with the matter."

"Ah, very good. Very good indeed. I believe I shall accompany you on your task," said the lord. "Yes, I believe I shall.

Perhaps I will have the opportunity to do some hunting during the ride."

Lord McConnell staggered to his feet, bellowing for horses and hunting dogs to be readied.

Lord McConnell's cavalcade arrived at the peasant's cottage without incident. And that was a problem. Deprived of his one great love, hunting, Lord McConnell further indulged his second love, wine. His retainers were amazed their lord could still ride.

Drawing up outside the cottage, the tax collector made to dismount, saying, "I'll just take care—"

"Peasants!" shouted the lord. "Your lord and master demands you stand before him and pay your taxes!"

The door to the cottage flew open as a man and boy hurried out to bow before Lord McConnell. "Please, my lord, I have given all I have! I beg you to allow me to pay an extra measure next month."

"My lord," the tax collector said, "this man's wife is the village healer. I believe she will earn well in the next month, as November always brings the first ill humors of winter. The man should have no trouble paying the extra measure."

Lord McConnell swayed in his saddle, gazing off towards the nearby forest. "Do you know the forest well, peasant?"

"My lord? I don't—"

"It is a simple question, one even a simple man such as you can answer," Lord McConnell shouted.

"Aye, I know the forest well, my lord," the peasant replied.

"Then I offer you a wager, peasant. If you win, you owe nothing more for this month. If you lose, I'll consider your offer of an extra measure in November," said Lord McConnell. "The wager is simple. You and your boy run into the forest. In five minutes, I loose the hounds and give chase. If you remain free when darkness falls, you win. If my hounds and I catch you, I win."

"But my lord—"

"Now go, peasant. Fly to the forest and give me the best hunt ever!" the lord said.

Everyone stared at the lord, aghast.

"Are you so confident, man?" asked Lord McConnell. "Your five minutes have begun."

Fear filled the peasant's face. Without another word, he grabbed his son's hand and ran off toward the forest.

"He runs well," mused the lord. "Huntsman, find something in the peasant's hut and give the hounds the scent. Perhaps this won't be a wasted day after all."

But Lord McConnell was wrong. The hounds treed the peasant and his son within twenty minutes. Angered at the poor quality of the hunt, the lord ordered them both taken to his dungeon. Having seen the man and boy chained to the wall in his dungeon, Lord McConnell repaired to his sitting room, where he tried to drown his anger with more wine. Instead, the wine only stoked the anger further.

Knowing well their lord's temper, his servants did their best to remain outside of his notice. Yet all heard Lord McConnell's anger build into rage as he paced the floor of his study, wine in hand, muttering and cursing. As the sun disappeared below the hills, the lord's fury overwhelmed him.

Staggering purposefully toward the stairs to the dungeon, Lord McConnell said, "Damned peasants! They rob me of taxes and of the joy of the hunt! Damn them!"

Lord McConnell ranted on as he descended into the dungeon. The servants heard the door to the dungeon cell open and slam shut. Then they heard the lord yelling and the peasants pleading. The yelling grew louder, the pleading more desperate. Then, the pleading turned to screams of anguish, then screams of pain. Screams that went on and on and on. Finally, silence fell and Lord McConnell emerged from the dungeon, blood coating his hands and clothing.

At that very moment, the healer woman, wife and mother to the peasants in the dungeon arrived at the castle.

"My lord," she said, holding out a jingling pouch, "I have begged and borrowed from the villagers and have the full measure of our taxes. Please, lord, where are my husband and son?"

The lord took the jingling pouch. "Come. I will take you to them."

Lord McConnell led the woman into the dungeon and threw open the door to the cell. The floor was red with blood. Trembling, the healer woman entered the room and beheld her husband and son. Both had been slashed and cut dozens upon dozens of times. Both had their throats slit wide open. Lord McConnell waited in anticipation for the hysterics to begin. For the second time that day, his peasants disappointed him.

The woman spun around to face Lord McConnell, her eyes blazing with rage. Instinctively, Lord McConnell fell back a step from fury.

"I curse you, lord," the healer said coldly. "I curse you to be hunted just as you hunted my husband and my son. I curse you to be hunted by hounds from Hell, chased until you can run no farther, and then ripped limb from limb! I curse you!"

Without thinking, Lord McConnell drew his dagger and plunged it into the woman's heart. As blood flowed from her wound, the woman smiled.

In a voice as cold as death, she said, "By my words invoked. By my blood sealed."

As her lifeless body dropped to the floor, Lord McConnell's hunting dogs bayed and howled. The sound ripped through his mind and clawed at his sanity. Staggering out of the dungeon, hands clasped over his ears, the lord ordered his huntsman to silence the dogs. When nothing the huntsman could do would silence them, Lord McConnell took his sword and slew them all.

From that day forward, Lord McConnell could not bear the sight or sound of any dog. Panic seized him should he hear a dog bark or see a dog in the village. So the lord issued orders that all dogs in his fiefdom were to be slain and none allowed to enter it.

Only after the grisly work was done could the lord sleep at night. And, slowly, his terror of the curse faded.

One year later, the curse all but forgotten, Lord McConnell reclined in his sitting room, relaxing after a fine dinner and enjoying a fine wine. Then, far in the distance, he heard hounds baying.

"Who has brought hounds into my fiefdom?" he demanded of a servant.

"Hounds, my lord?" asked the servant.

"Yes! Did you not hear them baying in the distance just now?" asked the lord.

"I heard no hounds, my lord," the servant replied.

Thinking, perhaps, it was the wind or his mind playing tricks on him, Lord McConnell settled back and took another sip of wine. The hounds bayed again. But this time, they sounded as if they were just outside the castle.

"Surely you heard that!" demanded the lord.

"I swear, my lord, I heard nothing!" replied the servant.

Then the hounds bayed a third time, this time from the castle courtyard.

"And now? Will you swear you heard no hounds now?" screamed Lord McConnell.

Backing away slightly, the servant gave no answer.

Then the lord heard growling coming from the far side of the room. Terrified, he looked toward the sound. Six pairs of glowing red eyes stared at him out of the shadows. Slowly, the eyes moved from the shadows and Lord McConnell once again beheld his very own hunting hounds. The hounds he slew one year ago. For they still bore the wounds Lord McConnell dealt them.

Throwing his goblet at the dogs, Lord McConnell cried, "Keep them away from me!"

"Keep who away from you, my lord?" asked the servant.

"The hounds! Keep the hounds away from me!" Lord McConnell screamed as he fled the room.

Baying, the hounds gave chase. Lord McConnell ran toward the dungeon, all the while pursued by the hounds. Down he ran. Down to the cell where the healer woman laid the curse one year before. Lord McConnell slammed the cell door shut, and the lord's servants heard him beg and plead for the hounds to be called off. Soon, his pleading turned to screams, and the screams went on and on and on. When the screams finally stopped, none of the servants would descend into the dark dungeon to discover their lord's fate.

The next morning, a guard went into the dungeon and opened the door to the cell. Blood splattered across the walls and covered the floor. Lord McConnell lay dead, ripped limb from limb.

Hundreds of years later, there are those who can hear screams coming from the dungeon. But those who have darkness in the hearts hear not the screams. They hear the baying of the hounds.

MR. FOX

M r. Fox was not known to the host and hostess, but She had no doubt he would be asked to join the soiree they held in honor of their daughter, Mary. Was Mr. Fox not suave and handsome and, from the cut of his clothes, obviously rich? He was the perfect suitor for their daughter, just as She intended.

Through Mr. Fox's ears, She had heard many proclaim Mary as the most beautiful young lady in the county. Now, She saw through Mr. Fox's eyes the truth of those proclamations. Mary was not merely beautiful, Mary was the most beautiful woman She had ever seen through Mr. Fox's eyes, more beautiful than any she had seen through Mr. Fox's father's eyes, more beautiful than she had seen through any Fox's eyes for over a hundred years.

Oh yes, this one will do nicely!

Mr. Fox, who was privy to all of Her thoughts and emotions, quailed inwardly while outwardly he gallantly kissed Mary's hand. He knew what She would want with this one. Oh yes, he knew.

Quite right, my pet, she spoke in his mind. Quite right, indeed! I will not be consuming this one. Not yet. This one you shall keep for me. With her, you shall bring a new Mr. Fox into this world. And when the time is right, he shall replace you!

She savored his horror as he relived the awful night ten years ago. The night when his father had presented him to Her. The night when She left his father and took him. The night when She made him kill his father and feed his mother to Her. And he despaired at the thought of the same happening to his own son.

But none of this was visible on his face or evident in his voice. She played Mr. Fox like a puppet, slave to Her strings, mouth to Her voice. He screamed and screamed, and none could hear it save Her.

Mr. Fox charmed and dazzled Mary; by his powerful physique, his well-appointed face, his gentle wit. It was soon evident to all that Mary was smitten by this stranger. After but a few visits, Mary's proud parents announced her betrothal to Mr. Fox. His screams echoed again, and She laughed and laughed.

She also hungered. As Mary would not be consumed for many years to come, She required other food. Mr. Fox announced to Mary that he must travel on business for a few days.

"Oh, but there is so much I do not know about you, my darling!" Mary protested.

Mr. Fox smiled his warm, gentle smile. "You will learn, my dear. As time passes, you will learn."

"At least tell me where we will live after our wedding!" Mary cried. "I must know what clothes to pack and what to send for later."

"I live not far from here," Mr. Fox answered. She knew there was no harm in telling Mary. No young woman of Mary's station would ever be allowed to travel the countryside unattended. "Half a day's ride to the west, there is a forest. Within the forest is a valley. Within the valley is my home."

Kissing her hands, Mr. Fox stood. "Now, dear, I must take my leave of you."

Mr. Fox rode out from the house and through the afternoon

and most of the night. The next morning he was married to Anna, a young woman who would be thought pretty unless she stood beside Mary. Mr. Fox quickly loaded Anna and her things into his carriage and drove off. He could feel Her hunger building. She made him return home all the faster that it might be sated.

Anna cooed over the valley as they entered it. The fine house enchanted her as they drove up to. Anna giggled as Mr. Fox swept her off her feet and carried her into the house. Mr. Fox headed straight for the stairs, so strongly did She call him to Her.

"Oh, let's not go upstairs yet," Anna said. "I wish to see everything about my new home!"

"You will see all you need to see upstairs," She made Mr. Fox say.

"Oh, you scandalize me," Anna replied playfully. "But I really do wish to see the whole house!"

Anna reached out and grabbed the railing, giggling again. But Her hunger was too great to wait even a moment longer. Through Mr. Fox, She drew his sword and cut Anna's hand off with a single slash. Staring at her bleeding wrist, Anna was too shocked to scream. Mr. Fox carried her upstairs, opened the door to Her room, and She came forward to feed. Then Anna screamed and screamed and Mr. Fox could do nothing to block the sound.

The next morning, Mr. Fox returned to Mary for their wedding. Mary and her family met him for breakfast. She did not look herself as she placed a covered plate before him.

"You look pale, my dear," She made him say. "Are you feeling well?"

"I am merely tired. I fear I did not sleep well last night," Mary replied. "I had a most horrible dream."

She forced him to smile lovingly, "Perhaps you should tell me the dream, my darling. Such dreams may be banished when brought into the light of day."

"I dreamed I went to your house," Mary said. "I dreamed a sign over the gateway read 'Be bold! Be bold!'"

Mr. Fox started in wonder, but She started in fear.

"It was not so, it is not so and, God as my witness, it shall never be so!" She made Mr. Fox say.

"When I came to the door to you house," Mary continued, "carved above it were the words 'Be bold! Be bold! But not too bold!'"

Once again, She forced Mr. Fox to say, "It was not so, it is not so and, God as my witness, it shall never be so!"

"I entered and climbed the stairs," Mary said, "and came to a door over which was carved 'Be bold! Be bold! But not too bold! Lest your heart's blood should run cold!'"

Mr. Fox felt hope, something he had never before allowed himself to do. And he felt Her dread at what Mary would say next. Yet She kept firm control.

"It was not so, it is not so and, God as my witness, it shall never be so!" She forced Mr. Fox to say yet again.

"And I opened the door, Mr. Fox," Mary said. "Within the room were dozens, maybe hundreds, of dead women. Blood splattered the walls. But something moved within the room and I fled. Do you know what I saw as I descended the stairs?"

"What, my love," he felt himself say. Dread, delicious dread, still coursed through Her, but Mr. Fox could feel Her overcoming it. He could feel Her regaining Her control. He could feel his brief hope flicker and die.

"I saw you, Mr. Fox! I saw you and a pretty young woman arrive in a carriage," Mary said. "I saw you carry her inside. I saw you cut off her hand with your sword. I saw you carry her upstairs. And I heard her screams as you opened the door at the top of the stairs!"

"Dreams can seem so real, my dear," She made him say. "But I assure you it was not so, it is not so and, God as my witness, it shall never be so!"

Then Mary lifted the cover off of the plate she had placed before him. Lying on the plate was Anna's hand.

Staring haughtily at him, Mary said, "It was so. It is so. But, God as my witness, it shall never be so again!"

Mary's brothers and father rose from their seats and struck Mr. Fox again and again with their swords. In Mr. Fox's head, She screamed and screamed and none could hear her but him. And, as the light faded from his eyes, he laughed and laughed.

ABOUT THE AUTHOR

Henry Vogel began his writing career in comic books way back in the 1980s, with the indie titles *Southern Knights* and *X-Thieves*. When the bottom dropped out of the black & white comic book market, Henry went into IT, where he worked for the next thirty-three years. Henry took up professional storytelling in 2006, and has performed all across his home state of North Carolina.

As a lifetime fan of science fiction, Henry always wanted to write science fiction novels. He began writing *Scout's Honor* in 2012, and released it to the world in 2014. He hasn't stopped writing since.

Henry makes his home in Raleigh, NC, and is hard at work on his next novel.

www.henryvogelwrites.com

ALSO BY HENRY VOGEL

Travis & Trouble
Trouble in Twi-Town
Trouble on Mars

The Fortune Chronicles
Fortune's Fool
The Scales of Sin & Sorrow

The Scout Series
Scout's Honor
Scout's Oath
Scout's Duty
Scout's Law
Scout's Training
Scout's First Mission
Hart for Adventure
The Princess Scout
Scout: The Lost Colony Adventures

Non-series books
The Lost Planet
Heart of Dorkness & Other Stories

The Connaught Family Chronicles
The Fugitive Heir
The Fugitive Pair
The Fugitive Snare

The Hostage in Hiding

The Captain Nancy Martin

The Counterfeit Captain

The Undercover Captain

The Recognition Series

The Recognition Run

The Recognition Rejection

The Recognition Revelation

Comic Books

Aristocratic Xraterrestrial Time-Traveling Thieves Complete Collection

Southern Knights Almost Complete Collection

Southern Knights Color Edition

Southern Knights: The Morrigan Wars

Southern Knights: Leaving Atlanta (prose novella)

Missing Beings

Illustrated Children's Book

I'm in Charge! and Other Stories

www.ingramcontent.com/pod-product-compliance
Lightning Source LLC
Chambersburg PA
CBHW030904200726
48289CB00003B/888